FALCO

For Erica

FALCO

Book I: Blurr and the Raging Horde

Daryl Periman

To order additional copies of this book, contact:
Xlibris Corporation
1-888-795-4274
www.Xlibris.com
Orders@Xlibris.com
106824

Contents

Chapter 1

The Falconer's Bird

The bells jingled as the peregrine falcon shuffled her legs up the gloved hand. Thin leather straps wound around each leg just above her taloned feet then dove down into the tight grip of her master's fingers. She stood proudly upon the fist, already savoring the feel of the wind in her face and anticipating a good kill. She was blind; the momentary loss of sight soothed her, kept her focus.

"There now," said the familiar gruff voice of her master. She felt her head being forced forward and down; white light shocked her pupils as the leather hood was lifted away.

Vast oceans of pine trees lay before her with a skirt of open sagebrush flats in the foreground. She cast a glance into the heavens noticing thin wisps of cloud hovering in the upper sky. *No cover for hunting today*, she thought. Small bells, like those used in Christmas decorations, hung from each leg and danced about with each fidgety step. She had gotten used to the ringing most of the time, but when hunting, the noise was not helpful in stalking her prey.

"It's going to be a good day to hunt Blurr," said the old man soothingly. "You know what to do."

The etched lines of the man's wizened face scanned her profile in admiration. She was a beautiful specimen, and very deadly. Her head was adorned with dark-gray feathers shaped like teardrops that draped over each side of her head. Gray cascaded down the back of her neck toward her tail, each feather outlined in white. Her keen brown eyes glistened, piercing through the helm of gray like an ancient warrior's. Black inch-long talons emerged from scaled yellow toes, curving like scimitars and accented with a serrated edge for cutting and slicing.

"Time to fly!" said the falconer as his arm rose into the air.

She extended her wings and flapped anxiously. She longed for the open sky but could not leave until permitted. The falconer had not released her; she would have to wait for his command. He was all she knew; she owed him allegiance although she could never really explain why she had a connection with the human. She knew they were not kin, but he was her family. She would always return to him after the hunt, always chose him over freedom.

Suddenly the hand released the leather straps, and she was rocketing into the open expanses of Wyoming sky.

Blurr called to the wind with a loud *kirrreeeee*, challenging the elements to ground her.

As if in response to her cry, a gust of wind struck her fully, blowing her askew. She quickly compensated with wing and tail, righting herself.

Now it's time to play. Blurr flapped hard against a headwind to gain altitude. She leveled into a windless lull just above a lonely cloud floating listlessly. Her narrow wings tapered to points like those of a jet fighter airplane. Her body wasn't meant to soar like many other raptors; hers was made for one thing.

She spun, inverting and tucking as she played in the warm air. Up here, there was no one in charge but her. She knew that falcons were not the biggest birds in the sky, nor perhaps, the most ferocious, but she did know that falcons are and have always been the fastest. No other raptor could even come close to her death-defying power dive, hitting her prey with precision. She knew that if pressed, she could kill a hawk in the same manner. Up here, for the moment, she had no master.

Blurr circled the cloud, using it for cover. Soon she spotted rock doves perched in a tree below. She decided to make herself visible.

"Kirreeee!" she screamed as she dove through the cloud like a sewing needle into cotton. The instant she popped out on the other side, a dozen doves burst off the branches of the tree. One dove broke from the rest of the group and wildly flew into open sky. *Clearly a mistake.*

At once, Blurr's senses concentrated into one single focus. Her eyes tracked the bird and her mind calculated its speed and trajectory. Without conscious thought, she adjusted her direction toward the bird, folded her wings, and dove. For a split second, the air put up resistance, but just as quickly, it broke its hold, rushing over her exquisitely streamlined form. *Faster!* She prodded herself and folded her wings even tighter against her body.

∞

Below, the falconer watched expectantly. "All right, Blurr, live up to your namesake," he whispered. He knew Blurr was young, but she was the fastest falcon he'd ever trained and he'd trained many raptors in his day. She was brash and confident and seemed to fear nothing. The falconer was proud of his bird. He protected her in every way and gave her comfort, regular food, and lots of attention. He wanted her to believe that she *was* the essence of an aerial hunter and the queen of the skies. Ed Riser was born and raised in these mountains; he knew the real world was full of predators that could get her, but he swore the day he plucked her from the nest that he would protect her from them.

Ed had trained several hawks in his time but was always partial to falcons. They were usually more temperamental and demanded more attention, but their hunting technique intrigued him most. Raptors are defined by their killing technique. Once seizing their prey, they use daggerlike talons to squeeze and pierce the life out of the animal. Falcons, however, add a twist, which makes them go faster than any other living thing under its own power.

The falconer remembered the day his friend, Perry Antonio Gomez, city cop and avid poker player, accompanied him to the field. "Okay, Ed," Perry said with a hint of his Spanish accent, "I give up, why do you need to use my radar gun?"

"She's almost adult size now," Ed replied. "I saw her go after this pigeon the other day. I've never seen anything like it!"

"Look," Perry said, reaching into his police cruiser as the radio squawked unintelligibly, "I'm gonna have to go soon."

"How do you understand a word they say on them things?" Ed drawled; his hearing was failing as he pushed a ripe seventy-nine years old.

"Sorry, Ed," Perry said with a large grin. "Police talk is not for old people like you, eh?"

Ed pulled up his pants and attempted to stand a little taller. "Even on my worst day, I could still beat the hell out of ya."

"Okay, John Wayne," Perry said, holding up his hands in submission. "I give."

Ed and Perry had been buddies for years. Ed didn't like old people; they were boring and mostly got offended at his sense of humor. He met Perry at a poker game one night; it was nice to have a cop as a friend. Ed was known to be casual with speed limits.

"There!" Ed yelled, pointing into the distance and grabbing the radar scanner from Perry's hands. "Here she comes."

Ed raised the black rectangular box by the handle and pointed it up toward his bird. Then he kicked a crate lying at his feet to one side.

Immediately, three white doves exploded from the crate and flapped wildly into the air, leaving small downy feathers in their wake.

Suddenly, the minuscule dot in the sky, which he knew was his falcon, dropped as if gravity concentrated suddenly at that one spot and yanked the bird from the sky. "Santa Maria!" exclaimed the police officer. "Would you look at that!"

Both men glanced at the radar's tiny screen, watching the digital numbers rapidly increase.

"She just broke 120," Ed said calmly while his friend let out a breath of bewilderment, "180 . . . 190 . . . 196 . . . Come on!"

"Two hundred miles per hour!" Perry screamed. "You've got to be kidding me!"

Ed just smiled as he looked up just in time to see his falcon collide with one of the doves. A dull thud and the white dot fell limply to the ground while Blurr swooped in a tight circle and landed out of sight. Ed knew she was having a well-deserved breakfast.

The policeman's radio crackled from the cruiser; this time, Perry cocked his head to one side while pressing a finger to his ear. "I've got to go, Ed," he said a moment later, "but that was amazing!

∞

Blurr loved the dive; she knew the pigeon didn't even see her coming. She could usually break the spine of her prey in one blow; she much preferred the clean snap of the spine or neck.

She saw stars for a few seconds after the impact, but the loud *crack* from the dove's body told her it was over. She flapped to recover altitude and gathered her wits. She felt pressured to find her quarry before scavengers and roving predators did.

As if on cue, a dark shadow swooped over the terrain below. "It's going straight for my kill!" she exclaimed in frustration.

Blurr turned her head just as a high-pitched call of a hungry hawk slashed across her ears. *I've got to find that dove!* She thought as she barrel-rolled, flew a tight circle, and spotted the white patch of feathers only feet below her.

∞

Blurr landed on the contorted body of the dove lying out in the open. With one foot planted on the ground and one foot gripping the soft tissue of the dove with her talons, she began to drag her kill toward a nearby bush. She felt her talons sink deeply into the dove, causing warm blood to spill out over her toes.

She was hungry, but now, fear and anger began to take hold. It was only a matter of seconds before the hawk zeroed in on her location. She was inches from the cover of the bush when a large dark shadow loomed over her. She ducked instinctively as giant black talons skimmed over her in an attempt to rip her head open. She let go of the dove and bounded into the air flapping hard. *No good defense on the ground*, she thought as she frantically scanned the sky for the next attack.

It came without warning. Blurr sensed a rush of air from above and belly rolled, flaring her talons toward the hawk. The hawk was not expecting this, as he too had his talons ready for shredding. Instead, his grip landed within the falcon's, instantly the four feet joined in a tight lock, neither bird letting go.

Unable to flap their wings, both birds spiraled while plummeting downward. "Let go!" screamed the hawk.

"You first!" Blurr retorted.

Neither bird made the first move and they were approaching the ground fast. Soon there wouldn't be time to pull up.

"I said let go!" the hawk bellowed again, this time in a more frightened tone.

"Not a chance!" Blurr yelled. She knew the first one to let go was the first one to open up to an attack.

With a loud grumble, the hawk loosened his grip and pushed away from her. Blurr instantly swiveled around to find green leaves smashing her in the face.

She heard a rapid succession of twigs snapping and felt her body being poked and struck in every location. She stopped with a jolt, feeling as contorted as her dead dove had looked moments ago.

Trying to gain some orientation, she heard thrashing noises coming from nearby accompanied by frustrated grunts and screeches of the hawk. *Ha! He met my fate as well!* A dark wave of pleasure filled her.

Getting one's own food, after all, is the most honorable way of eating for flying hunters. To simply steal another's kill was atrociously detestable.

She heard the rustling cease as the hawk managed to free himself from the bonds of foliage. "I'm claiming that food as my own, falcon," the hawk said with clear determination.

Blurr could only see the hawk's tail feathers from within the bush as he strode by, heading in the direction of the dove.

Anger swelled to boiling point, Blurr thrashed her entire body, feeling both wings free themselves and then her legs. She landed on the ground behind the hawk. "Not today," Blurr whispered through clenched beak.

The hawk pivoted to face her. "Leave now," he declared maliciously, "and I won't rip you!" He sized her up and determined they were nearly equal. He knew that if it came down to a scuffle, the falcon could possibly cause as much harm to him as he to her. A ripped wing or a broken bone meant death for a bird of prey and meant not an honorable death, but a death of starvation. If she didn't back down now, he would have to ramp up his bluff if he really wanted her kill.

"I said back down," the hawk said, ruffling his feathers and stepping closer. This would give him even a larger appearance.

"That's my kill," Blurr said, skipping sideways, attempting to block the hawk's path. "Are you a hunter or a pathetic vulture!" Blurr said, her words dripping with malice.

"You would risk death, chick," the hawk said, trying to keep his cool despite the insult. "To keep that sorry excuse for a meal as your own?"

"The answer is obvious," Blurr responded coolly. "Don't you think?"

A moment passed in silence; the hawk seemed to be thinking hard on his next decision. "Have it your way then!" The hawk said as he lifted off the ground, flapping hard and creating a commotion of dust and debris swirling in his wake.

Blurr watched the hawk's silhouette get smaller when suddenly a large black boot whooshed past her face and landed with a crash into a nearby bush. She stared at the wavering branches trying to process the odd object and how it came to be flying.

"Get away from my falcon!" yelped a voice breathlessly.

Just then, her master appeared, trotting with a limp through the bushes. "Ouch!" he screamed, grabbing his foot.

Regaining composure, he quickly grabbed his other boot. "Get outta here,"–the man stammered while he attempted to catch his breath–"before I let you have the other one!"

Ed surveyed the area looking for what he thought was going to be a major battle between his prized hunting bird and some rogue hawk, but all he found was silence. Some songbirds chirped happily nearby. He peered down at Blurr standing comfortably on her dove and staring up at him inquisitively.

"Guess my boot really scared him off," Ed said confidently, hoisting his trousers while tucking his disheveled shirt back into them. "You can thank my pitching days, Blurr, state champs '48-'49." Blurr noticed her master grabbing his shoulder and wincing.

Blurr didn't understand what her master said; there were only a few commands she recognized, but he looked content enough. She felt the breeze kiss her feathered face, her prize in her grasp, and suddenly she thought that the air smelled sweeter than before. Blurr had won this battle and earned her meal. She began plucking the angel-white feathers from the dove, the breeze carrying them away. She always felt comforted with her master close by, yet she could never completely trust him at the same time.

Chapter 2

A Photo Op

Liz Wheeling was a spry one-hundred-and-one years old and sitting in the passenger seat of her cherry-red Jeep Cherokee alongside a deserted road in Grand Teton National Park. Her hair was dyed jet-black, and she wore a bright pink sweater shirt and many gold bracelets on her wrist. Her skin was wrinkled and dark brown, like tanned leather. She loved the outdoors, and a century of sun was evident. She held a high-powered camera with a zoom lens in her lap. She never missed an opportunity to get a good wildlife shot to put in the local paper. Photography was her passion, and she had an eye for good shots. The only problem was that she couldn't walk as well these days and was restricted to taking pictures from her car, chauffeured by her daughter.

"Wait a minute," Liz said softly. "Pull up around that gate over there."

"Mother!" Her daughter, Annie, said, pointing, "There's a sign on the gate that says 'no public access.'"

Liz ignored her. She had a reputation for conveniently ignoring signs if it meant getting the picture she wanted. "Annie," Liz bellowed, "go around the gate, I need a moose picture."

"Yeah, right," Annie said under her breath. She knew her mother was hard of hearing; anything she wanted her mother to hear had to be said three times the normal volume. She pulled the jeep forward, inching her way around the posts while bushes and trees grudgingly were pushed aside as they passed. There was just enough room to squeeze through. "Oh, mother!" Annie shrieked. "The branches are scratching your paint!"

Liz was simply staring out the window, waiting patiently to get into the clearing ahead. Her camera bounced with the swaying of the car. She adjusted her grip, holding it soothingly.

"The light's fading," Liz said, scanning the scene ahead. "We need to hurry."

"Oh dear," Annie fretted, now driving down the empty road. She was already thinking of what to say if they were pulled over. *My mother's over a hundred, Officer, she's always wanted to see this place!*

Just then, Annie slammed on the brakes as a black amorphous blob the size of a beach ball flew directly in front of the windshield. The car lurched forward; Liz was caught by the seat belt. "Oh my god," Annie screamed. "What was that?"

"Back up," Liz said while she fumbled for another lens. "I think it landed in that tree."

"Was that a meteorite?" Annie asked as she put the car in reverse, looking back over her shoulder.

"Stop, stop, stop!" Liz yelled, pulling the camera up to her face and resting it on her door.

The late afternoon clouds had intensified the darkening of the sky, yet there was plenty of light to see a trail of broken branches that terminated at the base of an old pine tree. There, unmistakably present, was a dark mass that seemed to bubble and melt from the nearly spherical form it was just a moment ago.

Liz cursed trying to focus her lens. "Not enough light," she whispered.

Annie was peering over her mother, her hands on the wheel in case they needed to make a hasty retreat. "Annie," Liz said looking through her viewfinder, "drive closer."

$$\infty$$

Annie and Liz argued about the notion of getting closer to this thing. Annie contended that it could explode or exude a poisonous gas or at the very least stink up the car. Liz looked at her daughter coolly. "Annie, I love you," she said softly. "Now drive over there and make it snappy, I'm losing my light!"

Exhausted and defeated, Annie complied, driving just off the edge of the road and positioning herself only a few feet away from the blob, still bubbling at the base of the tree.

Through her camera, Liz watched the black tarlike substance begin to rise in the middle as if something were pushing from underneath. Now a spire standing three feet tall began to widen in all directions. The blob was taking shape, though neither woman could tell what it was becoming. Liz clicked her camera several times. "Oh, mother," Annie exclaimed in terror, "we better get out of here, I don't like this."

"Wait a minute." Liz said, attempting to reposition her hands. "Hold on."

Annie's palms began to sweat, making the steering wheel feel slippery. Seconds passed by, but it felt like eternity in her frightened state; the blob was no longer a blob but now took on a definite form. It also looked like it was breathing.

∞

"Annie," Liz said, putting down the camera and pushing the button to roll up her window, "drive!"

As if electrocuted into action, Annie jammed the jeep into drive and wheeled around, speeding down the lane. The gate was fast approaching, she would have to take it slowly again around the posts. Just then, a bang resounded within the vehicle, and the roof of the car caved in slightly. Both women screamed.

Reflexively, Annie hit the brakes and watched as an immense creature slid down the windshield and screeched to a halt on the hood of the car. Annie's mind was swimming, wings the size of a hang glider spread before her, shrouding the light. Liz and Annie were paralyzed in horror.

The eyes were large and completely void of color or pupil, but instead, glowed white-hot. An enormous snout baring a leaf-shaped nose at the tip grimaced to reveal glimmering white fangs, moist and dripping clear liquid. Thick jowls like a pit viper gaped as it hissed then bellowed a long hideous shriek that filled the car. The two women winced in pain, sinking back into their seats.

A strong scent of decayed flesh threaded its way through the cracked windows. Annie wanted to hit the door lock and roll the windows up, but not even her fingers could move. She felt as if someone cracked her head like a coconut and left it exposed to the elements and she couldn't command her body any more. She tried to extend her hand toward her mother in despair; panic filled her as she sat helpless in the driver's seat.

Annie realized that she was going to die; she was sure it was going to happen. She was certain that her mother was already dead, though she couldn't turn her head to see.

The monster's head began to waver on a long flexible neck; its blank white eyes fixed on Annie. A blur of dark was seen as the creature struck the windshield and Annie involuntarily screamed, and so did her mother. A spiderweb of cracks burst in all directions. Immediately, the monster recoiled, dazed and confused as to why it couldn't get to its prey. Annie felt her body return to her, and she slammed the door lock button and flipped the switch, closing all the windows.

"Mother!" she screamed. "You're alive!"

"Of course I am," Liz said angrily, pulling her camera up to her face.

Just then, Annie heard a siren. She didn't know if it was real or if she was imagining it. Light suddenly filled the space where the dark creature loomed. It had vanished. She saw a car pull up on the other side of the gate. A thick green band ran across its flank; she could just make out the words "Grand Teton National Park Ranger."

∞

Annie opened her eyes. A bright light was on the ceiling and the narrow walls were lined with bandages, syringes, and various medical equipment. She realized she was lying down on a small gurney inside an ambulance. A translucent oxygen mask was covering her mouth. The other bed lay empty and looked as if no one had been in it. She instantly thought of her mother. Why wasn't she in the ambulance too? *Oh my god, please no, please no, please no!*

The doors to the ambulance opened suddenly and a wave of panic and questions flooded her mind. She tried to ask about her mother through the mask, but the paramedic didn't hear her. He gave her a slight smile and a wink and grabbed a black box, leaving her alone again with the doors left open.

A wink!? Annie thought. *I'm lying here and my mother is out there somewhere and all he does is wink?*

"Okay," said a man's voice from just outside, "I'll get her."

Annie saw a man climb into the ambulance; he removed the mask. "How are you feeling, ma'am?"

"I'm fine," she announced impatiently. "Now, where is my mother!?"

"She's okay," the paramedic said quickly. "She's asking for you just outside there."

"Why isn't she *in here*?" Annie asked, her frustration rising.

The paramedic smiled sheepishly. "Well, ma'am"–he said, clearing his throat–"she didn't have a scratch on her, her vitals were good, and every time we tried to get her to lie down, she refused and threatened to hit us with her camera."

"I want to see her," Annie said, her fear subsiding. "Now!"

The paramedic helped her out of the ambulance. Annie stood in wonder. Lights, cars, conversations of dozens of people crowding the road were a far cry from the deserted lane she remembered earlier. It was now night time, many pairs of headlights filled the surrounding forest.

They strode over to the jeep. Liz sat inside on the passenger side, waiting. Annie opened the door and Liz reached out a tanned arm, drawing her close. "Annie," she whispered in Annie's ear.

"Yes, mother," Annie said tenderly.

"I need a drink."

Chapter 3

The Envelope

The door opened slowly. A small-statured gentleman in a gray suit poked his head through the door. Brad Pinkerton was sitting behind his desk working late that night; he always worked late. He looked up to see his messenger waiting for his permission to enter. "Come on in, Jonathan," he said with superficial enthusiasm. It had been a long day.

"It's here, Mr. President," Jonathan said, holding an envelope gingerly. The messenger walked briskly across the stately office carpet and put the envelope carefully on the desk. The president of the United States took the envelope with a sigh. "Thank you."

"Will you need anything else tonight, Mr. President?" Jonathan asked crisply.

"No," Brad Pinkerton said with a tired smile. "Go home, get some rest, and thanks."

The president had received word about some strange sightings in Wyoming of UFOs, monsters, and mysterious deaths. Usually, this is not something he would address, but the White House double-checked the sources and found that there might be physical evidence of something dropping out of the sky and getting up and disappearing into the wilderness.

Brad Pinkerton knew what could happen if this story was taken hold by the country at large. So far, it's just a small western town, with locals chanting scary stories. Just then, there was a knock at the door. "Come in," he said.

"Burning the midnight oil?" said a portly man in his mid-fifties with dark hair showing streaks of gray along the sides of his head.

"Same as you, Stan," Pinkerton said. "Captain of the ship has to stay as late as the crew, right?"

"Unless," Stan said entering, "he falls asleep on the job and sinks the boat."

Both men laughed as Stan flopped down on a gravy-colored leather couch sitting opposite the president's desk. "You look at the articles yet?" Stan asked, loosening his tie.

"Just got them," Pinkerton said, holding up the giant manila envelope. "Shall we?"

Stanley Nullfield, vice president of the United States, nodded as he watched his colleague and long-time friend open the envelope.

The first piece of paper he pulled out was a picture of an old woman with black hair and large sunglasses and with brilliantly white teeth smiling as she sat on a wicker chair. The caption read, "Liz Wheeling, long-time town resident, said the alien crashed into her windshield before disappearing."

"You're kidding, right?" Pinkerton said.

"Read on," Stan urged, now smiling in anticipation. "It gets better!"

Brad Pinkerton read through the article in its entirety. He read about the alien and how it came from the sky, changed shape, and flew off. He also read about the federal employee from the Grand Teton National Park who saw something fly off from the car but was hesitant to say what it was. The president then pulled several more articles, all within days of the first one, saying that a large dark flying object was swooping in people's yards taking household pets and small livestock. The ranchers couldn't blame the bears or wolves because the "critter was flying."

Brad Pinkerton relaxed slightly; he was becoming convinced that this was going to be only an entertaining headline that the public would soon lose interest in. Stan broke in, "It's the last one that caught my attention."

Pinkerton reached in to grab the last article. He unfolded it and shuddered as he read the title, "Child Taken, Valley's Monster Suspect!"

"Oh my god," said the president quietly. "If this doesn't get under control, we are going to have a nationwide panic." Stan nodded as if he had already come to this conclusion.

"Are you sure this is legitimate?" Pinkerton asked.

"I had my sources confirm the physical evidence," Stan said. "It's sitting in the basement of the town's police department's evidence room as we speak."

"And the child?" Pinkertson asked with hesitation.

"Still missing," Stan said. "Local authorities are not confirming or denying that an animal could be the culprit."

"What evidence do they have?"

"It seems," Stan said, now leaning on his knees, "the common denominator of all these sightings is a tar-like goo at the crime scene. This was found where the child was last seen."

"It could be a copycat," Pinkerton urged. "Or just some nut who read the local paper and is trying to hide his tracks."

"Sure," Stan said assuredly. "But then again."

"Damn," Pinkerton said, rubbing his temple. "I knew you were going to say that."

"It's my assigned job," Stan said with a wide grin.

Pinkerton rose out of his chair and turned to face the glimmering lights of Washington, DC, Stanley Nullfield also stood, grabbed his brief case he had set next to him on the couch, and waited. "Well," Pinkerton said, "let's get somebody out there."

"I already have my people assembling," Stan said. "A good team, I trust them."

"Stan," the president urged, turning to face his friend, "we've got to keep this quiet."

∞

At that moment, two men and two women were packing for a trip out west. The mission was to control a critical situation and keep it out of the public's eye. No one knew what the mission was yet, but they all knew it was personally assigned to them by the vice president and endorsed by the president himself. It was a big chance for all four Federal Bureau of Investigation operatives to shine in the line of duty, a chance to prove themselves with the president of the United States counting on their success. It was a chance of a lifetime; of course, none of the four agents ever thought that this chance would take place in Jackson Hole, Wyoming.

Chapter 4

Unsolicited Freedom

Blurr was sore from yesterday's hunt. Her underbelly ached and her right foot kept cramping up. She had had a terrible night's sleep and was cranky. Her master hadn't brought breakfast–usually one dead mouse, flawlessly white, raised in captivity, and downright scrumptious! He was late. She stood on her perch and hunched slightly to conserve heat as the cool night air lingered even though the sun had been up for an hour already.

Blurr anxiously sidestepped on her perch. She was surrounded by slats of pine, spaced about an inch apart to let in light and fresh air. Blurr thought she heard a bump and creak coming from the direction of the back door, hoping that was her master finally attending to her.

Blurr stared at the door; she envisioned her master shoving it open and holding a mouse by the tail, dangling like a furry pendulum. She heard a crack, like wood splitting, then suddenly a wave of heat washed over her. She backed away on her perch as much as she could go. Something was wrong.

From her perch, she could see her master's cabin and the back door he normally came through. Blurr continued to watch the door, willing it to open. Panic rose as she fidgeted; the bells at her feet jingled merrily. The heat was intensifying and she decided to drop to the ground where the cool earth comforted her slightly. Suddenly the birds in the surrounding trees went berserk.

Screams could be heard, both animal and human, then a wailing song as sirens cried from a long distance away. That's when the smell hit her.

A foul stench that burned her lungs led way to a thin trail of acrid smoke that slunk its way into her cage. Panic transformed to terror as the breath was sucked out of her and she saw flames licking the cracks of the cabin's back door.

The fire roared as windows smashed, and chunks of cabin flaked off as if the fire was alive and dismantling each log from within. Another intense heat wave coated Blurr like the relentless waves of the ocean. Each passing blast of heat forced her to inch further back in her cage until she was scrunching up against the wooden slats. She desperately stuck her beak through the nearest spacing and tried to fill her lungs with smoke-free air. She choked and sputtered as there seemed to be no clean air left to breathe.

Though she was young, a predator like a falcon is familiar with death. She sees death in the food brought to her cage, and she creates death in the food she kills. What clicked in her mind was perhaps the acceptance of her own death in these very last moments.

There was no air left to fill her, nowhere to go to escape the fiery wall of flame that was dancing around all four walls of her cage. It was only a matter of time until she either suffocated or burned to death. She realized her master wasn't coming to rescue her this time.

She heard voices yelling from the front of the cabin. The sirens were louder but dulled by the splintering of wood and the crack of flame.

"Over here!" screamed a fireman, dressed in full regalia, holding the head of a large hose.

The hose blasted huge amounts of water at the cabin's back wall. Blurr could feel the cool of the spray, but it did little to quell the flames now engulfing her cage. The heat was unbearable, whether a state of shock was gripping her or she had decided this was her moment to die, she did not know. *I am ready.*

A snap startled her out of her predeath trance. She peered at the ceiling in her cage. A board had cracked and given way. The desire for self-preservation lies at the core of every beast; when a chance to survive presents itself, instinct seems to take over, bypassing conscious thought and acts accordingly. Though Blurr didn't think through any plan of escape, she reacted immediately when the board fell to the ground in a flaming heap. She lifted off the perch, flapping hard against the current of super hot air tossing her body in every direction. Her tail constantly adjusting, her wings beating frantically, she rose toward the burning ceiling. It was going to be close. The space wasn't any bigger than her body, and now that she was there, it looked smaller!

Flames seemed to guard the exit with vicious vigilance by passing over the opening at regular intervals. She would have to time her retreat exactly or be lit on fire and endure a very uncomfortable way to exit this world. She drew one last breath and fluttered her wings as fast as she could. She closed her eyes at the last moment and launched herself through the opening. With her eyes closed, she could feel the heat caress her body with a sense of lament at the fact it couldn't grasp her and choke her. The smoke strangled her lungs and burned her from the inside. She couldn't tell if her wings were flapping or not, nor could she tell where she was going and whether she would land somewhere that wasn't on fire.

A sudden cool surface hit her face with a shock. She rolled through tickling grass until she stopped face up looking at the billowing clouds of dark smoke rising above her and catching a hint of direction from some unseen breeze. The constant crackling of fire on wood seemed more distant and less threatening, and the undeniably welcoming sensation of cool on her back was pure relief. She breathed slowly again and again until she could feel life seeping back into her. Blurr righted herself onto her feet and surveyed the scene around her. The cabin was charred and barely visible through the haze of smoke. If her master was in there, he was surely dead, and that meant she was on her own.

For falcons, sadness is different than in humans. Blurr regretted the situation, but her mourning for her master was one of immediate acceptance as the thought of survival gushed into her mind and overtook her. She couldn't dwell on his passing; she had to dig deep into her peregrine lineage, now she wasn't just on a hunt to pass the afternoon. Now, she was to hunt for survival in a world with which she has had very little experience. *Calm your fear, Blurr*, she thought to herself. *There's no one to protect you anymore.*

∞

Perry Antonio Gomez was second on the scene. No one saw Ed Riser come out of his cabin and his car was still in the driveway. Perry called Ed's cell with no answer. It was too hot to enter the cabin; the firemen worked frantically trying to keep the flames from reaching the nearby canopy of pine trees. Perry remembered where Ed kept Blurr; he rounded the cabin to find Blurr's cage completely swallowed in flames.

"What was in there?" said a fireman unraveling some coiled hose.

"My friend's falcon," Perry said regretfully. "I wish I could have at least saved her."

"You know," said the fireman, "I did see something fly out of there before it was completely charred."

"Really?!" Perry exclaimed. "It wasn't on fire or anything? Like it actually flew out?!"

"Well," said the fireman, "there was a lot of smoke, but I'm pretty sure it was okay."

Immediately, Officer Gomez ran to his police cruiser; he called dispatch and reported in. A fleeting thought entered his head and he asked Angela Tomsin, police dispatcher and known animal lover, "Angie, I've got a question for you."

"Go ahead," she said in a monotonous voice.

"If a wild bird was caught," Perry started, "raised in captivity, and then released, what would the chances of survival be?"

"What kind of bird are we talking about?" she asked, her professional voice changing to one of personal intrigue.

"A peregrine falcon."

"Call me on my cell," Angie stated quickly. "Dispatch out."

Perry did as Angie had asked. She told him that many people have the misconception that animals will simply pull out their instinct and do what their species has done for eons even if those animals were living in captivity since birth.

"But I've heard of people putting alligators in sewers and they grow up big enough to eat taxicabs," Perry interjected.

"Perhaps it's true with some reptiles, fish, and amphibians," Angie had said. "But birds and mammals require a significant amount of learning from parents to have a decent shot at surviving well enough to bear young. The slight nuances of tackling a large grass eater with horns without getting impaled is not necessarily instinctual. It comes from several trials of success and failure. Those that failed usually met death before reproducing. Those that succeeded would pass on their learning to the young. Each generation refining the technique and passing on what worked."

"Okay," Perry said now pulling into the police station parking lot. "If an animal missed that education because it was plucked from the wild or grew up in a zoo, you're saying it doesn't have a chance?"

"No," Angie said. "Its chances of survival are very low if it cannot find members of its own kind to coach it along. Acceptance of an outsider is tenuous and can sometimes result in the killing of the newbie."

"So there is still a fighting chance, this falcon could be alive out there?" Perry said, turning off the engine.

"Of course!" Angie said enthusiastically. "There's always a chance."

Chapter 5

First Impressions

A large commercial jet began to descend. The four members of the FBI peered out their windows. Long accustomed to the straight edges of buildings in the nation's capital, the team gazed out in awe. Gigantic rows of peaks stretched to the sky and were topped by plumes of threatening thunderstorm clouds. "Looks like rain," Mike Johnson said as he stared out the window.

"This place looks angry," Zoe Millman said from the next seat. Millman was the most petite on the team and it was deemed most appropriate that she sit next to Mike Johnson, a former football player whose broad shoulders could nearly fill two seats.

"Kurt," Millman whispered back down the aisle, "are you seeing this?"

"Yeah," Kurt Fitzpatrick said, poking his head into the aisle, smiling. "I wonder if we'll run into any cowgirls."

Millman shook her head; Kurt Fitzpatrick always had your back in tight situations, but he rarely took anything seriously.

The plane was coming in from the North. Patricia Nelson, the team leader, sat in silence as she looked out her window and saw a vast, open flatland covered in sagebrush until it hit a meandering river, patches of trees, then jagged pieces of rock looming menacingly like parapets on a giant's castle. The intercom chimed, "If you look out the right side of the plane, you'll see the mountain range called the Tetons."

"Hey, Patricia," Fitzpatrick said over the seat in front of him where his team leader sat next to an elderly man, "Tetons, that's French, right?"

Nelson rolled her eyes; she appreciated his sense of humor, but sometimes, he just wasn't as funny as he thought. "Yes, Kurt, it's a French word."

"Thought so," Fitzpatrick said with feigned innocence. "Do you know what it means?"

Here it comes, Nelson thought. "Didn't you take French in high school, Fitzpatrick?"

"Oh yeah," Fitzpatrick said disappointedly. "I forgot I told you that already."

Millman, who was sitting two rows up, overheard the conversation. "Okay," she said, talking through the space between her seat and Johnson's. "I give, what's Tetons mean in French?" She could see Patricia Nelson's face easily, sitting directly behind, a look of "just don't ask" flashed across her face. She saw Fitzpatrick's face appear between Patricia Nelson's seat and the old man's. Only a vertical snapshot of his mouth, nose, and middle forehead could be seen. She watched as Fitzpatrick silently mouthed the word "boobs," then his lips stretched into a huge, toothy grin and disappeared from view. Millman leaned back in her seat, rolled her eyes then giggled in spite of herself.

"What are you laughing at?" Johnson asked in his clear, deep, serious voice.

"Nothing," Millman said quietly. "Nothing worth mentioning."

Patricia Nelson continued to look out the window; she had been in the agency for almost ten years, had successfully accomplished many dangerous missions, and had been in command of countless agents. She felt very assured of her skills and her team's skills. But she couldn't help the nervousness that welled inside of her. The "call" she received concerning the nature of the mission was disturbing and vague. Mysterious disappearances, evidence of extraterrestrial life-forms, globs of goo at the crime scene–they all sounded ridiculous. Now that she was here, the open expanse of mountains became a stark reminder that she was a city girl and that this mission was going to be hard.

∞

The Jackson Hole Airport is one of the only airports found within the boundaries of a national park. The surrounding mountainous topography meant unpredictable weather. A storm loomed above the jagged peaks; the landing was bumpy. Patricia Nelson had to hang on to her armrest tightly in order to focus on not losing the ham sandwich she ate for lunch.

The plane lurched to a halt next to the only other plane on the tarmac. After it stopped, numerous seat belts clicked as people unclipped and began gathering their belongings. It was clear as everyone stood up that she and her three agents were unaccustomed to the West, especially Johnson. Being a huge black man–with dark sunglasses, bald head, six feet six inches of muscle wearing a perfectly ironed collared shirt, tie, and black pants with leather shoes–he stood out the most.

"First thing I'm going to do," Fitzpatrick said, grabbing his hand bag, "is get a cowboy hat."

"How about you?" Millman asked Johnson playfully. "You going to get a cowboy hat too?"

Johnson didn't smile. He just looked down at the small woman. He raised one eyebrow and in a deep voice said, "It'll mess up my hair."

Millman giggled and walked off the plane with the others. Two men, two women, all four now wearing long black trench coats and sunglasses got off the plane with fifty-three other people, most of whom were already snapping pictures of the scenery and ogling an arch made of elk antlers as they entered the airport.

The four agents looked at each other. "Well," Nelson said, raising both eyebrows at the archway as they entered the main terminal, "guess we better change clothes."

Normally, agents of the Federal Bureau of Investigation arrive on an assignment fully dressed and geared for the backdrop. Each agent had received the "call" only minutes before the last flight for the day to Chicago left, making connections to Jackson Hole. Each tried their best to bring an assortment of clothes as no one had ever been to Wyoming and didn't quite know what to expect.

They entered the airport to a host of people greeting long-lost friends, some veering over to the rental car counters or scanning the battalion of chauffeurs for one holding a card with their name; some drivers were dressed as if they just stepped off the set of a Western movie.

"Look!" Fitzpatrick said enthusiastically, pointing to a man holding a large sign with several names scribbled on it wearing a large black cowboy hat with matching leather vest and a huge handlebar mustache. "Do you think I should get a black cowboy hat?"

"Yes, definitely," Millman said in a serious tone walking next to him. "I think the bad guys always wore black hats."

"You're hilarious," said Fitzpatrick sarcastically.

"Oh yeah," Zoe Millman said with a smile. "I'm funny."

Word must have preceded them as a Jackson police officer stood conspicuously by the doors leading into the terminal. His eyes scanned the crowd shrewdly then locked on Johnson as he passed through the doors. The officer approached Mike Johnson as Patricia Nelson intercepted the cop.

"Hello," the tall officer said politely. "Are you from DC?"

"Yes," Nelson said cautiously. "Why you do ask?"

The policeman was courteous and mentioned that he had received orders to welcome them. He also said his captain was waiting for them at the station in town. The officer escorted the four agents to a small room off the main terminal; there, they were joined by an older athletic-looking gentlemen dressed in jeans, a flannel long-sleeved shirt, and a "Jackson Hole" baseball cap. His hair was gray, but his blue eyes met each agent's gaze with confidence and sincerity.

"Welcome to Jackson Hole," he said happily. "I'm Ray McCullen, airport director."

They all greeted with handshakes as McCullen explained that their firearms could be checked privately as directed by a phone call from the vice president of the United States.

"At first," McCullen said, "I thought it was a joke. But when I heard the vice president's voice list off my military history, commending me for my service, let's just say I was convinced."

"Thank you," Nelson said congenially, "for allowing us to maintain a lower profile than we anticipated."

"My pleasure," McCullen said with a sincere smile. Ray McCullen had flown everything from bombers to fighter planes; he was in his sixties and winning triathlons in his age group. He loved his job and loved the fact that he could help his country again. The police already confirmed the coming of the four FBI agents and the need for some special treatment. The phone call from the vice president was pure bonus.

They went outside to the curb. The officer offered a police escort into town, but Nelson thought that would look too conspicuous and opted for a regular taxi. Nelson noticed many onlookers staring at Mike Johnson with a mixture of curiosity and suspicion. "I'll get a cab," Johnson said as he held out a massive arm to hail the nearest taxi.

There was a line of minivans across the lane; the driver of the first one in line was leaning against his vehicle. He saw the large black man hold his hand up. The driver, wearing jeans, t-shirt, and an old straw hat, stood rigid, blinking as if pondering his next move. Nelson stood beside him and yelled over, "Are you a taxi?"

The man nodded absentmindedly. Johnson lowered his hand and looked quietly down at Nelson who stood at his chest level. She looked up at him. "Better get used to that, I guess," she said consolingly.

The taxi driver made no motion to come and pick them up, so the four agents hoisted their minimal luggage and walked across the lane.

Kurt Fitzpatrick sensed the driver's apprehension as they approached the minivan. "Johnson," he said loud enough so the driver could hear as he put their bags in the back, "looks like there's not enough room back here, better sit shotgun."

Zoe Millman giggled as she and Fitzpatrick climbed in the minivan's side door, followed by Nelson who flicked Fitzpatrick's arm as she sat down.

Mike Johnson filled the passenger side completely, his knees pushing against the dashboard while his head bowed slightly against the ceiling. The driver tenderly got into his seat and closed the door. He tried to resume a face of casual indifference as he looked into the rearview mirror. "Going to town?" he asked, his voice cracking.

"Yes," Nelson said. "To the police station please."

The driver went rigid again then looked at Mike Johnson sitting next to him, his bulging arms only inches away. Johnson turned his head slowly to face the driver, his sunglasses on. Expressionless, he stared silently at the driver for a moment. The driver turned pale and seemed at a loss for what to do. The FBI agent slowly turned his head back to face front again. "We're not paying you by the hour," he said calmly. "Are we?"

Instantly, the driver shifted into gear, faced forward, cleared his throat nervously, and drove out of the lot.

Chapter 6

A Trio

Blurr had just made her first successful kill as a wild falcon. She stood upon the dead grouse, a larger bird than her normal prey. About the size of a chicken, grouse are fat and clumsy flyers; the amount of meat was worth the hard impact. After plucking feathers and gorging on the warm flesh, she was already full. *There's so much left!* she thought.

She hesitated as to what to do; there was a lot of meat left. Should she just leave it and hunt again later, or stay and defend the carcass from anything that happened to catch the scent?

She tried moving it—the idea of taking it up to a tree branch seemed like a good one, but the weight of the bird and her full stomach made it impossible. She loved the hunt, but her head was still spinning from the impact on the grouse, the thought of hunting for her next meal when there was a perfectly good, and already dead, meal here was more desirable at the moment.

A rustling in the canopy of a nearby stand of aspen trees caught her attention. Fear leaped to her throat. She didn't see anything but the waving of branches and leaves, yet she felt like she was being watched. Her keen eyesight scanned every contour, looking for movement; the leaves were distracting like they were purposefully trying to hide something.

"So," a tiny voice asked casually, "are you going to eat the rest of that?"

Blurr jumped into the air and, without thinking, flew to the nearest branch of an aspen, landing clumsily. She swiveled her head side to side, sweeping the view for the source of the voice. The intruder was here, but where?

"Who are you?" Blurr asked, trying to keep the nervousness out of her voice.

"Dot," replied the small, squeaky voice.

Blurr pivoted on the branch, shifting her feet in the direction of the sound, bobbing her head for better focus, desperately trying to identify her stalker's location. She found nothing, although the voice seemed closer than before. *It must be moving in for the kill!* she convinced herself.

She needed to keep it talking. "What are you?" she said in the general direction she determined her adversary was hiding.

"What am I?" it asked incredulously. "It is none of your concern, simply know that I am larger, smarter, and far more vicious than you ever could be!"

"Really," said Blurr suspiciously. "Then show yourself."

"Listen to me, little birdie," squeaked the voice laced with confidence. "If I revealed myself to you, it would be too much for your pebble-sized intellect to handle. I could not have that weighing on my conscience."

Blurr was getting frustrated. She felt like the tiny voice was practically squeaking in her ear as if she could reach out and touch the source of it. It was unsettling to have such an annoying yet powerfully elusive thing insulting her with no target for retribution. She decided to lift off; she crouched and leaped off the branch. As she did so, her wings brushed against something that was soft, not anything plantlike. "Hey, watch it!" screamed the small voice.

Blurr glanced back and saw movement as she was pulling up. It was small and almost indistinguishable amongst the backdrop of bark and twigs and leaves. She kept her eyes fixed on it as she wheeled around. *Now I have you, little one.*

The little owl saw the falcon coming, his bright-yellow eyes widened in horror as Blurr zeroed in with lightning speed. He didn't have time to react; he just clacked his beak then stepped back off the thin branch where he had been staging his performance. Blurr adjusted for the oncoming branches, dodging and weaving occasionally, snapping twigs as she dove through the canopy after the little creature.

The owl bounced off branches. "I . . . *thwack* . . . can . . . *bump* . . . explain . . . *thwump*," piped the owl as he hit his way down, eventually landing on a large branch only feet from the ground.

Blurr immediately pounced on him, each taloned foot straddling his teacup-sized body. She peered down at him. "Okay, little *birdie*," she said venomously, "explain then."

"Okay," the owl said nervously. "First, I'd like to apologize for insulting you . . . and your intellect."

"Go on," Blurr urged.

"I'm also sorry," he continued as he looked into her fierce gaze with fright, "for startling you, it was rude and impolite and . . . please don't kill me!"

At that, Blurr's body relaxed slightly. She had never had any real interaction with other birds except the ones she killed for food or battled with when they would try to take her food. She didn't know what else to say or how to respond to his plea. She never really thought of killing the little creature; she just wanted to teach him a lesson.

"I'm not going to kill you," she said quietly. She stood more upright, realizing she had been mantling over the frightened owl. A moment later, the owl righted himself. "Thanks," he said, ruffling his feathers and then deflating them smoothly.

Blurr stood facing him; he was so small. She had never thought owls came in this size. "What kind of owl are you?" she asked curiously.

"I," he announced with pride, "am a Saw-whet owl, but you can call me Dot."

"Saw-whet?" Blurr asked.

"It's a human thing," the owl said dismissively. "Apparently, I sound like the noise a tool makes when it's wet."

Blurr looked at him in confusion; the owl noticed. "I don't really get it either, safer just to be called Dot."

Dot was mottled with gray and black, while flecks of rustic red ran down his body. She could see why he blended in so well. *An excellent choice of feathers for hiding.* His yellow eyes were expressive of his mood as his lids would rise and fall when he spoke.

Suddenly, a large dark shape flew over the tree. Its form was partially hidden by the canopy that waved above them. Blurr crouched, watching intently. Dot froze, blending into the bark of the tree. The aspen's bark was mostly white, but there was enough brown for his camouflage to be effective. They both stood still, waiting.

The shadow circled back over the tree. Blurr could tell it was large; the wingspan was much bigger than her own. She remembered the dead grouse she had killed earlier and thought that if the bird became distracted with her kill, she could leave unnoticed. Nervous seconds ticked by with only the shadow to see in view.

From the viewpoint of the lower branch, little could be seen but the ground directly ahead. Blurr could, however, see the grouse lying unattended. Just then, a giant black bird landed near the grouse. Its head popped into view, pink and featherless. *A vulture*, Blurr thought in disgust.

She had never met one, but their appearance was revolting, their lack of real talons was pathetic, and she felt they weren't worth getting to know. She noticed Dot instantly relax beside her.

"Whew," he sighed. "That was nerve-racking, wasn't it?"

Blurr looked down at him; she didn't quite know what he meant. She didn't feel threatened by the vulture; however, she thought Dot, being so small, would be threatened by it.

"Don't worry," Dot said, peering out at the vulture. "That's Ralph."

"You know him?" Blurr asked, surprised.

"Yeah," Dot said, his wide eyes reflecting his contentment. "He's my buddy."

"Buddy?" Blurr asked tentatively.

"You know," Dot said, "friend."

Blurr thought she understood the concept of master and servant and predator and prey, but friendship was a mystery. She was quickly realizing that her captivity sheltered her from more than just hunting daily or protecting herself. "What does 'friend' mean?" she asked.

Dot looked surprised. He gazed at her genuine expression and determined she wasn't joking with him. "Well," he began slowly, "'friend' means that you're together because you want to be."

"And Ralph," Blurr said, nodding toward the vulture who was now devouring chunks of grouse meat and swallowing them whole, "is your friend because you *want* to be around *him*."

Dot nodded happily. "He's not very bright," he said. "Actually, he's dumber than this tree here, but he's loyal and makes me laugh."

Blurr watched in revulsion as the vulture had plowed his head fully into the grouse's midsection, jostling and tugging, then rising with streaks of blood and particles of flesh clinging to his face. She felt repulsed and could not imagine wanting to be around this vile creature.

"Do you want to meet him?" Dot said suddenly, pulling Blurr out of her trance.

"I don't think so," Blurr said slowly.

"Oh, come on," Dot pushed. "He's not dangerous."

"I'm not afraid of him," Blurr said with more annoyance than she intended. "I need to be moving on, that's all."

"Look," said Dot softly, "you're a big, majestic falcon, I'm small, and he's ugly. I can see why you wouldn't want to hang around us, but . . ."

"But what?" Blurr asked.

"But," Dot said, his eyes narrowing slightly, "I'm guessing you could use a friend . . . or two."

Blurr felt hurt and embarrassed at the owl's comment, but the truth was that she *was* lonely since her unintended freedom only two days ago. It was amazing that she was surrounded by living things. The whole sky was open to her, yet no one seemed to want to be around her. Birds flew away, and anything on the ground ran for cover or didn't care if she was there or not. The only one who ever filled that void was her master. She didn't know how to be a friend to any other living thing.

Dot stood patiently waiting for a reply. Blurr looked at the owl then at the vulture then back at the owl. "Okay, let's go."

"Great!" squeaked the owl jubilantly. "Oh, hold on. You better let me go first, he gets really nervous sometimes and has the tendency to throw up."

"That's gross," Blurr said, trying to keep the vision out of her mind.

"Tell me about it," Dot said rolling his eyes.

Blurr waited, watching the small owl flutter out to greet his friend. The vulture met Dot enthusiastically; they talked for a moment, then Ralph's pink head went erect, and he nervously surveyed the area. It appeared to Blurr that Dot was still talking when she saw the vulture's leg begin to stomp the ground like a dog being scratched in just the right place. Only Ralph's face was not that of pleasure but of pure fear.

Dot turned to Blurr and waved her over with his little wing. Blurr leapt off the branch and flew close over the ground landing gently next to Dot. Ralph froze; his mouth slightly open, he said nothing. The vulture just stared as if suspended in time; his wings slowly began to unfold until they were spread to reveal a six-foot wingspan. Blurr watched curiously, wondering what the vulture was going to do.

"Ralph," Dot said soothingly, "fold your wings in, please."

Ralph, face still frozen, began pulling his huge wings back in. Dot whispered, "Stay, Ralph, stay." Dot took a step closer to the nervous bird. "Good, Ralph."

"This is—" Dot began when he stopped suddenly realizing he didn't know the falcon's name; Blurr broke in.

"Blurr," she said quickly.

"Blurr," Dot repeated slowly. "Ralph, meet Blurr. Blurr, meet Ralph."

Blurr nodded silently, fixed on the fearful expression of the pink face looking back at her. "I'm Ralph," he finally choked out.

"Well," Dot said loudly, "now that we've all met, let's eat!"

Dot immediately grabbed a hunk of meat and swallowed, ignoring the vulture and falcon who both continued to stare at one another. Blurr had no desire to eat anymore, but the silence was uncomfortable; she didn't know what to say.

Suddenly, Ralph began to convulse; his head bobbing up and down as if he had lost control of it. Blurr took a step backward; Dot looked up from his feast.

"Oh no," Dot said quickly. "Just look away, Blurr."

It was too late, Ralph had already thrown up a massive quantity of grouse flesh, bloodied and coated in slime; it came to rest at his feet. He looked up as if he was coming out of a trance and had just woken up realizing what happened.

Dot looked at Blurr as if to say "what can you do?" and said, "I told you he gets nervous."

Chapter 7

Rise of the Enemy

"I'm telling you," said Sherman Hinkley, geologist for a local surveying company in Wyoming, "I've found something significant!"

"Look, Sherman," said an older man with a graying handlebar mustache and dark expression, "I hired you to find minerals, not scout for melting glaciers."

Sherman put a handful of rolled-up maps on the man's desk. "I know that," he said, "I've only looked around on my own time but—"

"But nothing," replied the surveying firm's manager. "You are not using our equipment to dig holes in ice!"

"Don't you see?" Sherman said, pushing his glasses back up to the bridge of his nose, "The glacier has receded, we won't have to dig through ice . . . it's at the ice's edge where I found the cave."

"So let me get this straight, son," the old man said, stroking his mustache and leaning back in his chair behind the desk. "You want valuable digging rigs, man power, and my time to go searching for what you think is an ancient cave with some new life-form that we've never seen before?"

Sherman stared blankly at his boss; he knew Tom Bartlett was a hard man in the field but had a soft spot for Sherman, a geologist with lots of enthusiasm who loved to debate the identification of a stone and had a really good track history of finding valuable mineral deposits for mining. Bartlett leaned forward, putting his hands flat on the desk. He sighed, "Okay, you go up there and get some pictures, then we'll talk about getting famous with your new discovery."

Sherman beamed, scooped up his maps, and left Tom Bartlett's office before the old man could change his mind.

∞

It was late, he knew, but Sherman Hinkley was determined to get up there as soon as he could. He grabbed some maps off his desk, a water bottle, and some snacks and shoved them all into a backpack. He slid it on his shoulder and left his house.

The drive was beautiful in the late afternoon; sunrays spread across the valley and there was a warm stillness that was comforting. The Teton Mountain Range loomed on his left as he drove down the only highway toward Grand Teton National Park. He pulled up to the entrance.

"Good afternoon," said a young woman in her twenties wearing a park uniform as she stood in a small kiosk with a sliding window left open. Sherman nodded and smiled, handing her his park pass and driver's license. She stole a glance at his face then returned both items with a broad smile.

"Will you be needing a map today, sir?" she said, already holding one in her hand.

"No, thanks," he said, shoving his license back into the glove compartment. "Not this time." And he drove off.

As Sherman hiked the trail to the glacier, he thought about all the evidence there was about global climate change and how even raising the world's temperature by a couple of degrees might have drastic effects on plants and animals. He had been monitoring one particular glacier nestled between two huge cliff faces that seemed to always protect the glacier from the sun. He remembered finding the opening to what possibly was the entrance to a larger chamber, from what he could tell.

"That's not our business unless you found minerals," Tom Bartlett had said when Sherman first brought it up weeks ago. "Besides, it's a national park, and we can't mine in there anyway!"

"This could be more important than finding minerals," Sherman continued, talking more to himself. "I think the opening has just been thawed, if I could get up there–"

"Not on my clock!" exclaimed Bartlett.

Sherman tried several times to convince his boss that minerals *could* be up there, though the real reason for Sherman's interest was what he saw coming *out* of the cave.

He didn't believe in a "valley monster," but he did see something exit the cave that was big, black, and disappeared into the trees. It was only a glimpse, but Sherman knew it was something real and possibly never before discovered. He had checked the hole after it left, which was only two feet in diameter. What was even more exciting though was that he found hair.

∞

Soon the sun would be down completely, Sherman was prepared to stay the night to watch the hole for anything unusual. Just then, his cell phone vibrated in his pocket. Reception would be lost soon; he decided to answer it.

"Hello," he said, hearing static crackling in his ear.

"Hey, Sherm," said the faint male voice. "We were . . . meeting . . . Dornan's . . . what . . . you dork!"

"Sorry!" Sherman yelled into the phone; he had forgotten that he was meeting his friend Daniel Simms for a beer at a local tavern. "I'll be back tomorrow."

He wasn't sure Daniel could hear him, there was more static, a couple of unintelligible words, then the signal was lost. He would just have to explain later; Daniel would understand, he was a local science teacher and had been on many "Shermanating explorations" as he called them.

The woods didn't frighten him; he'd camped in areas where bears would wander through his campsite, or he could hear wolves in the distance. Up here, he knew the bigger animals wouldn't hang around due to the lack of plants and fresh water. Mostly some birds and small mammals lingered on this rocky slope. He thought about seeing the mystery creature he had only caught a glimpse of before; he felt that, like most animals, if he wasn't threatening and was vigilant, he would be okay. Suddenly, Sherman saw the dark opening peeking at him ahead.

He crouched low and took off his backpack. Setting up a small tripod with a video camera equipped with night vision, he peered through the viewfinder to make sure it was set on the hole. Darkness was settling into the mountains and the temperature was dropping quickly. Sherman pulled on a fleece jacket and got comfortable next to the tripod. He had a remote in his hand so he could press the button and start recording if he saw anything.

His belly rumbled, and he pulled out some beef jerky. He began gnawing on it when he noticed the only sound he could hear was that of his own chewing. *Strange, the birds and insects are quiet.*

A snap of twig made Sherman jump; his heart raced. The night seemed darker than a moment before, and he suddenly felt exposed and vulnerable. *Relax, Sherman. You're freaking yourself out,* he thought to himself. He took a couple of deep breaths and decided to press the remote's button. He could hear the camera switch on and begin to record.

Sherman decided to check the camera to make sure it was still centered on the dark hole only fifty feet away. He peered through: nothing. He put his hand on the camera to make a slight adjustment when he felt something sticky on his palm.

His looked at it inquisitively; it felt like tree sap, but even in the dying light, he could plainly see it looked like tar. *It wasn't there a minute ago.*

Sherman's face felt hot and flush as adrenaline made his body ready for action; the hairs on his neck pricked and his eyes were wide with fear. *Dark tarlike substance found at the crime scene* was all he could remember in the newspaper article.

Instantly, a large glob of the same tarlike goo dropped onto his hand. It was warm and encased his hand quickly, holding it in place and glued to the camera. Sherman looked up.

A dark mass moved slightly within the black shadows of the tree's canopy. It moved smoothly, like a mirage, shifting position so that Sherman had to allow his eyes to adjust in the darkness to even get a fix on its position.

"I'm not alone, get out of here!" he screamed into the branches. Panic was surging through his body and his trapped hand was beginning to sting, like a thousand ants were biting it from within the goo. The pain was becoming more intense by the second.

The shadow moved closer; this time, Sherman could see two softly glowing orbs become visible in the darkness, like headlights of a small vehicle. They hovered only feet from his head, suspended in motion.

Sherman felt like a fly trapped in a spider's web. The adrenaline was in full effect, the fight-or-flight response engaged, and Sherman grabbed the tripod with the camera attached; his hand remained fixed to the top of the camera. He swung the tripod toward the two glowing spheres.

"Get away!" he yelled as he banged the tripod's legs against the tree trunk, making a loud pop.

The eerie stare of the glowing lights didn't waver; suddenly, Sherman's head was filled with a vibrating voice. *Must change*, it whispered.

Sherman made more clanging with the tripod; this time, he screamed, cursing the looming darkness. His hand felt like it was on fire, but even more than that, the thoughts that entered his mind next made his legs buckle. *You will be mine.*

The attack came swiftly. Something hit Sherman from behind, striking him in the knee and caused him to buckle and land on all fours with his hands splayed out in front of him. He rose only to receive another blow that struck him on the back of his head. The sting was intense, as if someone were holding a blowtorch next to his skin. He reactively put his hand on the wound and felt the warmth of blood flowing over his hand. He felt dizzy and cold and shaky all at once. He couldn't seem to make his legs move while the ground beneath him began to sway like the rocking of a boat on rough seas. He collapsed, hitting the cold earth hard, his glasses flung from his face. Needles poked and grit scraped his cheek, but the rest of his body was numb.

The darkness was all consuming; he wasn't sure his eyes were even open anymore. A rotten odor of decayed flesh entered his nostrils, and more vibrating thoughts entered his mind. *It will happen soon.*

Sherman's hair blew back as a huge gust of wind swept dust and debris into his face. The wind ended as, a moment later, he could hear footsteps coming nearer. Black ooze dribbled near his face; the smell of rotten meat intensified.

He could hear breathing, thin and raspy. Sherman squinted, his eyelids being the only things he felt he could move voluntarily; the illuminating glow of the blank eyes was now close enough that they, themselves, provided light to see the features of an ominous face. Dark ridges in smooth skin and protruding mouth outlined in fangs filled his field of view. Sherman saw a leaf-shaped nose and a snakelike neck disappearing into a dark body.

Like a shroud of darkness, huge black wings encased him; the head dipped low beside his ear, Sherman heard the creature breathe into his ear, "You will join me and my horde."

Sherman's numb body was like baggage now, lifeless; only vague images of his life danced within his mind as the world filled with clicking noises, rapid and high-pitched. Sherman's vision faded to black, but not before he caught a glimpse of hundreds of pairs of glowing eyes staring at him from within the dark canopy of trees.

He didn't understand what the creature meant: "You will join me and my horde"; he only wanted to succumb to his fate and be gone from the pain and helplessness that he felt. Sherman withdrew any will to live; he only hoped it would be over soon.

Chapter 8

Invasive Species

The queen stepped away from Sherman. The body lay motionless; the hunt was too easy, the prey too helpless. *I remember now how easy it is to turn these animals,* she thought confidently. *I've been away far too long.*

Suddenly, she winced. A searing pain tore through her head; she couldn't control her thoughts, which meant she had lost control of her servant horde, which was now airborne and circling Sherman Hinkley. Huge looming shadows in the night scattered in random directions over the vast expanse of ice and rock.

Pain! She vibrated intensely to her servant horde; a deafening scream echoed down the mountainside as they all lost control, crashing in large black heaps on the slanted ice of the glacier. Their bodies instantly slid out of control, abruptly hitting the rock field in tangled piles of leathery wings at the end of the ice flow. The queen looked for the source of this power over her, something she had never encountered before; that's when she heard the music.

A fast-beat tune of drums rang out from the location of the prone body of Sherman Hinkley. The music repeated itself; the pain returned with as much intensity as before. The queen did not understand how this defenseless creature's voice could have such control over her as she and her children writhed in agony.

Then the music stopped suddenly.

We must retreat, the queen vibrated the idea in all directions. *Go, my children, to the nest!*

In the moments of silence, dozens of black shapes took flight as best as they could; like a mob of giant bats they fluttered, circled, and without losing speed, zoomed into the small dark hole in the ground one by one.

The queen lingered at the entrance, glancing in disbelief at how this animal could emit a signal that she could not interpret.

"Sherm!" entered the vibration into her mind. "Where the hell are you?"

The queen doubled over as if being stabbed in the belly; her head was splitting again. She attempted this time to locate the signal with more focus. In a crouched position on the edge of her nest's entrance, she swiveled her head quickly from side to side, large membranous ears fluttered as they attempted to track the signal.

There! She vibrated, her glowing white eyes burning hotter and narrowing; the signal was not from her quarry but from just underneath the body.

∞

It was getting late; Daniel Simms sat on a barstool waiting for his friend Sherman Hinkley to join him. *Sherman is rarely late, and he usually calls if he is*, thought Daniel.

"Can I get you something?" asked the bartender, a young man with a long ponytail streaming down his back.

"Not yet," replied Daniel. "I'll wait for my friend."

The bartender nodded and walked away, cleaning a glass with a dishrag. Daniel tried the cell phone again; the first time, he only heard something about "tomorrow." This time, there was static at first; he blurted into the phone, "Sherm! Where the hell are you?" then heard a shrill scream mingled with what he thought sounded like wingbeats of many large birds. *What is Sherman up to now?!*

Daniel tried again, but the signal was lost. He would call back every few minutes with the same result. The bartender approached. "Are you ready for something now?" he asked with a tinge of annoyance.

Daniel shook his head and stood, grabbing his jacket. He went outside to the parking lot, a clear sky full of stars; the Tetons erupted in the distance like dark shadowy centurions standing guard at their posts. Daniel sat in his car; he called Sherman's home and work with only voice mails answering the phones.

"Hey, Sherm," Daniel said to the automated voice mail, "I know you won't get this until you get back from wherever you went, but call me as soon as you can."

Daniel turned the ignition and pulled out of the parking lot, hoping his friend was okay.

∞

Daniel Simms walked into his classroom the next morning where high school kids waited for him as they chitchatted in their seats. Some acknowledged his entrance with a glance, others remained locked in conversation. Daniel decided not to worry about Sherman unless he couldn't make contact later in the day. It was not uncommon for Sherman to disappear then show up later with some crazy adventure story.

He stood in front of the class quietly; he scanned the room for missing students. It was the end of the year and he could easily search for absent kids by a glance. He noted that two were missing.

"Okay all," he announced, "let's begin."

Students began settling in by getting spiral notebooks and pencils out, the conversation dying down. "We've been talking a lot about this idea of evolution," Daniel began. "How a living thing has to have the right physical traits for the surrounding environment in order to survive."

Some kids nodded, others just stared blankly. "But what about living things that come from somewhere else," Daniel continued. "Ones that did not evolve in that area, what happens then?"

"You mean invasive species?" shouted a young blond girl from the back of the room.

"Exactly," Daniel said.

"Well," the girl said, "they either adapt to the new environment, move on to someplace else, or die out."

"Excellent!" shouted Daniel. "So if they stay, they better have the tools for the environment or perish, right?"

Several students agreed, then a boy in the front row with long dark bangs dangling over his eyes, raised his hand. "Yes, Miles," Daniel said, pointing, "do you have a question or comment?"

The boy smiled. "Okay," he started, his voice cracking slightly. "If a species comes in and takes over, if they have the right stuff to survive, is that a bad thing?"

"Well," Daniel said, "I don't think we can judge if its 'bad' or 'good,' it's just that whatever was living there already will be affected by this new species. The outcome of that effect might be good for some, bad for others."

The discussion continued throughout the class. Many students argued that if a plant or animal had the right tools to thrive in an environment, then that species should be allowed to stay. Others argued that invasive species ruin environments, forcing those that already live there out or into starvation. Daniel had fun moderating the lively discussion until his cell phone started vibrating in his pocket.

"Okay, folks," Daniel announced, pulling out the phone and looking at the number. "Let's turn to page 154 and take a look at a case study on this topic." He strode over to his desk. He knew the only people to call while he was in class were his kids or wife, both knew it could only be for something urgent. He didn't recognize the number, but something told him to answer it anyway.

"Hello?" he said softly.

"Mr. Simms?" replied a woman's voice. "This is park dispatch. Do you know a Sherman Hinkley?"

"Yes," Daniel said full of trepidation. "He's my friend."

"Mr. Simms," said the woman, this time she tried to sound more consoling. "Park rangers found your friend. He had been mauled by an animal and was taken to St. John's Medical Center."

"Oh no," Daniel exclaimed loud enough that many students looked up. "Is he in stable condition?"

"It was reported that it was pretty severe," the woman said. "I don't know more than that."

"I'll get over there right away," Daniel said quickly. The woman on the line asked if Sherman had family as the rangers could not find any other contacts except Daniel's number, which was the last call received on Sherman's cell phone found under his body. He told her that Sherman's mom was the only living relative and was in a retirement home. He would notify her himself.

"Can I have your attention please?" Daniel said to the class as he looked up at the large clock on the wall. "The bell is going to ring in two minutes. You need to read chapter 5 for tomorrow and outline the main ideas." There was some grumbling and shuffling of books. "What's going on, Mr. Simms?" asked a tall redheaded girl from the front row. She noticed his look of grave concern.

"I don't know, Mallory," Daniel said quietly. "I really don't know."

Chapter 9

Flight Lines Cross

Blurr had been eager to fly among the crags of high cliffs of the nearest mountain range. *A high perch will feel good, I think*, she thought.

Dot and Ralph had decided that they, too, wanted to fly toward the mountains, which just happened to be in the same direction she was going. Blurr surmised that their attraction to her was primarily based on her ability to find and defend food. Having longed for company, she decided that was fine with her for now, even if one of them was a vulture.

"Do we have to fly so high?" breathed the little owl as he pumped the air laboriously.

Blurr looked back and saw that he was going to need a break soon. "Just to those cliffs, Dot," Blurr said. "We'll rest there."

Ralph was lumbering high above them, easily soaring with barely a wing beat, his dark body teetering back and forth as he made small adjustments to the wind currents. "I hate it when he shows off," Dot said between breaths, catching a glimpse of his friend.

Blurr thought about her companions; it was the first time she hadn't felt lonely since the fire. But this feeling was different than what she had felt with her master. There was a bond with him to be sure, but not one of friendship, more of ownership. The man was her master and thus owned her; she responded to his commands obediently because she knew nothing else. She wondered now that if she had time to grow up in the wild, would she have acted differently as a falconer's bird?

"Okay," Dot wheezed, pulling Blurr out of her train of thought. "I'm done."

They had reached the shadows of the Teton Mountain Range and Dot was already on his descent. Blurr could see Ralph begin his as well, a slow series of descending concentric circles. It was amazing how fast she could cover distances. She began dreaming of all the lands that must be out there for her to discover.

"Hurry up you two," Dot yelled from below, the descent to the tree line giving him more confidence. "The light is fading."

Blurr dove hundreds of feet in seconds; she swept up at the last minute right behind the little owl just as they reached the cliff's edge. "Hey, stop that," Dot blurted. "Anyway, I totally saw you coming," he continued, trying hard not to sound startled.

Blurr chuckled as she gracefully landed on the rocky outcrop, Dot settling next to her.

"You better give him some room," Dot whispered as Ralph was preparing to land next to them. "He's not the best at landing."

Blurr was just scooting over when there was an earsplitting scream from the trees below; Ralph, having been very focused on his cliff landing, jumped and fluttered wildly, his concentration blown. It was too late; Blurr and Dot were bowled over in black feathers as Ralph careened into them, knocking them back into a small recess in the rock.

"Sorry," Ralph said apologetically, untangling his feet from the rest of the group. "What was that?"

"I don't know," said Dot, ruffling his feathers and peering over the cliff's edge. "I've never heard anything like that before."

Blurr joined Dot and scanned the forest below. They were at least three hundred feet up from the treetops but Dot could see perfectly well; most raptors are born with keen eyesight and are able to discern minute detail from vast distances. Owls, however, have the addition of seeing in very low light as well.

"You're a night hunter," Blurr said, turning to Dot. "Surely you must have heard this sound before, isn't it some kind of owl?"

"If it is," said Dot warily, "it isn't from around here."

Ralph had now joined them, stepping nervously to the edge of the cliff. He peeked over the rocky precipice. "How come there aren't any bugs?" Ralph said slowly.

As darkness encroached upon the cliff face, Dot turned to Blurr with wide, fearful eyes. "He's right," he said quietly. "No bugs."

"So," Blurr said confused, "I don't understand."

"It's completely quiet down there," Dot said, leaning over the edge, straining to hear even the slightest sound or see movement of any kind.

The usual sounds of the night were strangely silent tonight. Insects chirping, night birds, and animals hooting or scurrying about for food were absent, only a deep quiet and sense of dread hung over the forest. "I don't like this," Dot said with tension in his voice. "Not one bit."

For day hunters like Blurr and Ralph, flying at night is dangerous. Their eyes are not made to distinguish the shades of grays and blues of night; thus, the chance of collision is great.

"If you want to move on," Blurr said with annoyance, "then go, but I'm staying here." The last thing she wanted was to hold somebody back; she was starting to feel as if she had been held back all her life.

"Are you crazy!" Dot exclaimed, looking back at her with surprise. "No way I'm going, too spooky."

"But you're an owl," Blurr blasted. "A night hunter!"

"Yeah," Ralph interrupted, pulling back from the edge. "But he's afraid of the dark."

Dot extended a little wing and thwacked Ralph on the leg. "I told you," Dot cried, "not to tell anyone!"

"Sorry, Dot," Ralph said, moping. "But Blurr is our friend, we can tell her stuff, can't we?"

At those words, Blurr felt a surge of euphoria; a warmth of good feelings filled her entire being. She had never felt anything like it before, and she couldn't explain why she was feeling it now. The only thing she knew was that she liked what Ralph said about her being a "friend."

∞

The silence was suddenly broken by a sound they all recognized.

"Get back!" Blurr commanded as she swept her companions back into the rocky recess with her wings.

The oncoming noise could have been mistaken for a rush of water on a nearby river; however, the only river in the area was very far off. Blurr, Dot, and Ralph knew that sound came from hundreds of wings beating in the air at the same time.

Blurr stood in front of Dot and Ralph, her wings still outstretched like a protective shield. Dot peeked under one wing while Ralph hesitatingly looked over the other.

It was dark now; there was no hope of seeing anything. The stars twinkled overhead like an audience waiting for the show to begin. "Whatever happens," Blurr whispered, "stay here, move back as far as you can, and keep quiet."

Dot and Ralph acknowledged her with nervous grunts; Blurr could tell fear was overcoming them.

Ralph began his nervous twitch of stomping one foot erratically. The tapping of foot on rock normally wouldn't project much sound; however, to Blurr, it seemed like a giant beacon giving away their position. Dot caught on too. "Ralph! Your foot!" he said in a raspy whisper.

Ralph blinked. "Sorry," he said, forcing his leg to hold still. Blurr could see that it was difficult; Ralph only managed to keep it from tapping on the rock while the rest of the leg continued to tremble.

"Can you hear that?" Dot said urgently. "It changed direction."

"Which way?" asked Blurr, fearing the answer.

"Ours," Dot said.

∞

Blurr's heart pounded so hard she thought the other two could hear it.

She could feel a cold draft of air being made by wings pushing their way up the cliff face. "Stay here!" Blurr boomed.

There was no way she could defend herself properly backed into the tight cliff face. She hopped to the cliff's edge; below was a black sea of swarming movement with hundreds of glowing pairs of eyes rushing up the cliff face.

She leapt off the edge, flapping rapidly to gain altitude. The air was cool and, under other circumstance, would have been refreshing.

At least up there, I will have a chance of outrunning them.

"C'mon!" she screamed at her pursuers.

The response to her call was overwhelming; a chorus of screams and clicks that seemed to reach out and pull her down like invisible tentacles. She felt slow and heavy; her gaze began to drop earthward.

Blurr realized she was barely flapping; the dark mass of creatures was nearly upon her. She looked up at the stars and focused all energy she could muster and flapped her wings. The cool dense air allowed her to gain height quickly; she spotted a cloud and angled toward it.

"Catch me"–she whistled loudly–"if you can!"

She was hoping that most, if not all, of these night hunters were following her and did not notice Dot and Ralph tucked away in the cliff pocket.

Without looking back, she could sense that many dozens of flyers were following her to the cloud. She had an idea.

Blurr dove into the cloud; she was blind and hoped she was going the way she wanted. The screams and clicking sounds were right behind her and tracking her every move. She banked up deep into the bowels of the cloud; feeling her feathers dampen with moisture, she barrel rolled and angled straight down.

Tucking in her wings and dropping through the cloud, she dove.

A moment later, she could feel large bodies zooming past her in the mist. She banked right and left, narrowly dodging one dark shape after another. She smiled as she heard multiple collisions behind her. Her closest flyers had met the trailing stream of other dedicated hunters. She heard several grunts and sharp hisses, then something struck the side of her head as if she had smashed into a tree trunk.

She lost her breath. Choking for air, she tried to regain her balance, but it was impossible.

Blurr couldn't feel her body except for tingling that touched every fiber of her being, as if she were being electrified and numbed at the same time. The blackness she saw before her was speckled with flickering points that danced in front of her eyes.

She lashed out with her talons and dug deeply into soft hairy flesh. A high-pitched wail of pain engulfed her as both bodies tumbled out of control. Though she couldn't focus with her eyes, she sensed the body was much larger than she, heavy and cumbersome.

"Back off!" she cried, instinctively pumping her wings and trying to pull away. She released her talons, retracting her legs slightly and pushed off the hairy mass.

Blurr couldn't tell at first how far up in the air she was, only the sense of gravity told her which way was down. She attempted to right herself and began to flap. She only regained some orientation when she was suddenly hit by branches of trees that swallowed her into their tangled mesh.

Chapter 10

Enemy Ensnared

Blurr opened her eyes. She was staring up through boughs of pine tree branches; a soft purple hue was evident in the sky above, signs that dawn was approaching. She felt the knobby protrusions of bark poking her in the back. *I'm tangled in branches again?* she thought to herself, remembering the encounter with the hawk.

"That was amazing!" said a hushed raspy voice in her ear. "I've never seen a day shifter fly at night."

"Yeah," replied another raspy whisper, only this one was an octave lower. "The way it plowed through those things . . . fantastic!"

"Shut up," said a third whisper urgently. "It's moving!"

Blurr stretched one leg, flaring her toes; she could see that her black talons were still intact. Retracting the leg and following with the other one, she could hear gasps all around her. Her vision was clear, but her head was stuck; a dark pine branch on either side kept her in a fixed position.

"Wings are moving, Dad!" blurted the lower whisper.

Blurr could detect scampering of feet as she extended her wings; she was relieved to find both relatively pain free. She lifted her head out of the crook of the two branches and carefully swiveled about to stand firmly on the pine bough.

Light was gradually streaming through the canopy; Blurr was very much not alone.

Before her stood three large ravens, about equal in size to herself; they had positioned themselves with one in the middle and slightly higher than the other two. Dark and glossy with sparkling brown eyes, they froze, staring back at her, blinking.

"You all right?" asked the middle raven looking down at her.

Blurr nodded. Though her body was drained and her muscles felt sore, she seemed to be undamaged.

"I'm Dad," continued the middle raven, "and these two are my sons, Right and Left." Each bird nodded as Dad aimed a beak in each direction. "Don't bother trying to tell them apart." They all looked identical to Blurr as she peered at each one of the dark birds.

"I'm Blurr," she said, nodding. This was her first personal encounter with ravens. She had seen them many times while hunting; they always came across as loud and boisterous. They mostly ignored her when she hunted except once she had come too close to a nest of theirs. They saw her as a threat; they joined forces and mobbed her for two miles. Since then, she had always attempted to avoid them if possible.

Just then, the tree erupted in a violent shudder. All four birds flared their wings to keep balance on the branches. It felt like the tree itself was shaking like a wet dog, then they all heard the piercing scream.

Wincing, Blurr adjusted her position to get a better look upward. There in the topmost boughs was a dark, massive animal. It sounded like it was in a lot of pain. The ravens began making a loud cawing cry that was almost as abusive to the ears as the bat's scream of pain. A moment later, the screaming stopped, the ravens died down and settled, and the tree ceased quaking.

"Right, Left, go up there and investigate," said Dad like an old military commander.

"But Dad," said Left, "it's as big as an eagle and twice as ugly!"

"And," exclaimed Right, "I'm pretty sure it wants to have us for breakfast!"

Dad looked at his sons with impatience. "Well," he said as if it was obvious, "then be careful!"

Blurr saw both ravens attempt to come back with a retort, but thought better of it and started cautiously bounding up the tree branches. Minutes passed, Blurr had lost sight of the two ravens; they were too far up into the labyrinth of pine boughs to distinguish their shapes. She could, however, still see part of the looming black shape of the giant bat. It was now motionless.

"I don't think it's dead yet," echoed one of the ravens. "I can see its ear twitching!"

"I think the knock by the falcon really injured it," said the other.

There was a moment's silence; Blurr could hear the ravens moving around up there. "I dare you to go poke it!" said one of the brothers from above.

"That would be Left," Dad said to Blurr rolling his eyes as he looked up. "Will you two stop messing around up there and bring me back your report!"

The tree jostled slightly as the ravens made their way down the branches; they seemed less cautious and were rapidly whispering to each other.

The raven they called Dad was ignoring them at the moment; instead, he was fixed on Blurr's feet. "What are those?" he asked with deep interest.

Blurr looked down; she had forgotten about her falconer's bells. They were worn and weren't nearly as jingly as they had been only a week ago. The two young ravens joined them. "My master put these on me," Blurr said quietly, remembering the day she got them. She had felt very proud to have them then.

"They're very pretty," Dad said, blankly staring at them, mesmerized by their golden luster. The other two ravens also gazed upon them in a similar manner.

"Thanks," Blurr said slowly. She didn't understand the attraction; in fact, she would love to be rid of them. She was not a falconer's bird any longer.

"Why do you have them on you?" Right asked innocently.

Blurr told them of her captivity, her master, and the fire. The ravens listened with extreme interest, hanging on every word and occasionally croaking or cawing in excitement.

"My chicks could get those off of you," Dad said soothingly, "if you didn't want them anymore."

Blurr was surprised as to why any wild bird would want them, but the offer was enticing. She didn't have time to reply before the tree began to shake again.

"What . . . did . . . you . . . find . . . out?" Dad said, his voice shaking with the swaying tree.

"It's all," Right said with the same trembling voice, "tangled up."

"Yeah," Left repeated, "tangled. Big time!"

The tree suddenly stopped quaking again; this time, Blurr noticed heavy breathing coming from the creature. She knew what it felt like to be tangled in branches. She had no affection for the beasts that tried to kill her last night, but there was a twinge of empathy for this flying hunter being trapped up there. Thinking about last night, she suddenly remembered the cliff face.

"Listen," Blurr said quickly, "I've got to find my friends."

She had forgotten about Dot and Ralph until now; feeling a little guilty, she felt this sense of urgency to get to them and make sure they were okay.

"Wait!" cawed Dad. "Your bells, can we have them?"

"Maybe next time," Blurr said. She wanted the bells off; they were a reminder of her life in captivity, one that she now wanted to forget, but she felt she had to find Dot and Ralph. That was more important to her. She could not linger any longer.

Blurr stepped out on the end of the low-hanging pine bough, attempting to find a clearing where she could get enough space for lift out of the forest. "What about that thing?" she asked turning to face the three ravens.

"Oh yeah," said Dad casually. "We're going to tie it up."

"Why?" Blurr asked, thinking that would be the last thing she would do.

"Because," Left said as if this should be clear understanding, "we've got nothing else to do."

Blurr shook her head. It was clear she did not understand ravens. She turned on the spot and jumped off the branch. Flapping quickly and dodging a few branches, she was above the forest looking down at the tree. From here, she could see clearly the creature that she had collided with last night. It was even bigger than she thought; the sun shone upon it revealing that the hairy midsection was indeed a dark brown. The wings were mangled, but Blurr was surprised to see a shimmering dark purple fluorescence emanating off of the wing's membranous skin, like that of a duck's plumage.

She saw that the eyes were closed and the head was tilted back as if it was relaxing in the morning sun. Blurr circled one more time; she wanted to study the creature a little longer. She wanted to know this new enemy better.

This time around, she saw the puncture wounds made by her talons. Four holes in the abdomen, dried blood surrounding each entry point. She noticed that though it had a similar body to that of a bat, this large creature differed mostly in the face. It reminded her of the face of a wolf, only at the end of the snout was a leaf-shaped nose, thin and erect. It moved similarly to the twitching ears.

She had just finished her second pass when she saw the ravens approaching the ensnared giant bat; she didn't know how they were going to tie it up—she didn't want to know. Her empathy grew for the creature as she imagined it spending any length of time with those ravens.

Blurr pressed on, flying toward the mountains, attempting to retrace her flight path back to the cliff as best as she could. She was amazed at how different the world looked from day to night. Only moments passed and she could now see the gray crags of the cliff in the distance, she would soon find out if her friends survived the night.

Chapter 11

New Recruits

Daniel Simms arrived at St. John's Medical Center, a plush hospital accented with a Western motif and lots of cowboy and mountain paintings. The receptionist greeted him warmly; she pointed him in the direction of Sherman's room. "Thank you," Daniel said and walked briskly down a long carpeted hallway.

The door was ajar. "Hello, buddy," Daniel said as cheerfully as he could, knocking softly on the door and forcing it to open slightly. There was no answer; he peered inside the room. It was a typical hospital room—white walls and floor with an elaborate metal-framed bed; there was, however, a large window with a majestic view of an empty green valley surrounded by mountains. The hospital in the town of Jackson was set directly next to a traditional wintering ground for thousands of elk who had long vacated to the higher country for the warmer months.

Daniel entered, seeing that the empty bed looked as if someone was in it a moment ago; there was a cup of liquid in a closed plastic jar with a giant straw sitting on a small bedside table. Just then, the toilet flushed; Daniel wheeled around to see Sherman coming out of a bathroom. Their eyes locked in surprise.

"What took you so long?" Sherman said with a huge grin, coming through the door. He was wearing a hospital gown; his head and one leg were wrapped in bandages with cross hatchings of multiple scratches decorating his face.

"Sherm," said Daniel, feigning a serious look of concern, "you look like hell."

"True," Sherman said, briskly gesturing to the window as if he was unveiling something extravagant. "But I've got a nice view."

Sherman limped over to his bed, dragging an IV line hanging on a stand with wheels; he sat on the edge of the bed and pointed to his face. "You think the chicks will dig these scars?"

Both men laughed, though Sherman looked painful when his did so. "Sherm," Daniel cut in seriously, "why were you up there?"

"You're not going to believe it," Sherman said excitedly as he settled into his bed. "You know how I've been talking about that glacier melting away, right?"

"Yeah, but I don't get—"

"Wait," Sherman interrupted. "Some animals go into hibernation for the winter like bears or some species of ground squirrels. But some animals can literally freeze solid like our local frogs do. So what if an animal was frozen, like under a glacier, then all of a sudden the ice pulls back, the ground warms up, and the animals wake up?"

"Hold on," Daniel said, trying to put the pieces together. "You're saying that you think there is some animal that was frozen under that glacier and has now thawed out?" Sherman nodded excitedly. He adjusted his gown and lay back on his bed; he winked, and with a press of a button, the head of his bed began to rise. Daniel smiled, thinking how childlike Sherman acted sometimes; he liked that about his friend.

"So," Daniel continued, "that glacier's been up there for a long time. How long do you think these animals have been frozen?"

"Funny," said a woman entering the room. "I was just going to ask that same question."

∞

Daniel and Sherman looked up as four people walked quickly into the hospital room, two women and two men. One of the men was a huge, well-built African American wearing sunglasses. Daniel stood before them; his brow crinkled in confusion. "Who are you?" he asked suspiciously.

"My name is Patricia Nelson," said the woman. She wore a white collared shirt, shoulder-length brown hair that was graying, and blue jeans. Daniel guessed that she was in her fifties but looked like she could handle herself. She pulled out a badge and flipped it open. "We are from the FBI and are currently investigating what Mr. Hinkley has seemed to have encountered last night."

Sherman had already sat up and was trying to pull his rather loose gown around his exposed legs while improvising more coverage with the bed sheets. "You came for them?" Sherman asked tentatively.

"That's correct," Nelson said in a businesslike tone. "These are agents Johnson, Millman, and Fitzpatrick." Each agent nodded accordingly. Daniel noticed they were all wearing pretty much the same attire as Patricia Nelson, only the agent named Fitzpatrick was sporting a huge black cowboy hat.

"I'm Daniel—"

"Simms," Nelson cut in. "We know that you are a friend of Mr. Hinkley and work at the local high school. Listen, we don't have much time and I need some information from Mr. Hinkley, and I will also need something from you too, Mr. Simms."

Nelson sat on one of the guest chairs; Agent Millman closed the door and continued standing with Fitzpatrick and Johnson.

"Now, Mr. Hinkley," Nelson pulled out a small notepad and prompted, "tell me what you saw."

∞

An hour later, the four FBI agents prepared to leave the hospital. Sherman Hinkley had recounted last night's encounter with as much detail as he could. He also detailed his theory about the receding glacier setting in motion the release of these creatures. Patricia Nelson tried to remain passive when Sherman said that he saw hundreds or perhaps thousands of eyes that night. She knew now that this wasn't going to be a problem that could be fixed quietly if there were more than a few of these giant bat-like animals flying about.

Leaving Sherman to rest, the four agents and Daniel left the room and were walking down the hallway when Nelson turned to him. "Mr. Simms, I'm going to need to ask you for a favor."

"Sure," Daniel said. "What can I do?"

"Actually," said Nelson, "it's not you we need the favor from, it's your wife, Erin."

Daniel listened as Agent Nelson described how that if they were to capture or kill one of these creatures, they would need to learn more about it quickly and quietly. Daniel's wife was a veterinarian at a local clinic and would have equipment and knowledge to deliver this information. Daniel also found out that the FBI had studied both his and Erin's past history. They knew she had experience with exotic animal medicine and that they both had worked with various species of wildlife.

Daniel left the hospital, his mind racing to process all that he had learned in the last two hours. He also was wondering how he was going to break the news to Erin that the FBI wanted to enlist them in the capture of a creature that hadn't been on the surface of this planet for unknown eons.

Chapter 12

Friend or Foe

Blurr was almost to the crags of the cliff. The sun shone upon the rocky face, giving the impression of a peaceful rest stop. *Far from it*, thought Blurr. She angled down then swooped to the cliff's edge where she, Dot, and Ralph had all perched before the oncoming of the giant bats. She could see before she landed that it was empty.

Dread filled her. The loss of her companions washed over her mind, leaving it desolate and cold. She scraped around the outcropping looking for signs of her friends and what may have happened to them, but nothing but bare rock was visible, not even a feather.

Blurr peered over the edge of the cliff; the forest was green and vibrant with animals noisily going on with their day. She felt it was safe to make her own call. *Perhaps they are nearby*. She repeated her cry several times, a high-pitched short screech, one she thought would travel the wind and be picked up by Dot or Ralph. She waited in silent minutes; only the warm breeze could be heard as it rustled the pine needles below.

∞

It was a cloudless morning flawed only by the contrails of a jet flying high overhead. With regret, she left the rocky ledge, wondering if Dot and Ralph were still alive somewhere. She didn't know where to go, where to search for them. If they were taken by the night hunters, then they were surely dead and devoured by now. She felt like she needed open space to feel like she could see vast distances in all directions to feel safe; her keen gaze ever watchful for a vulture and a little owl.

She was flying over flat plains of sagebrush with the mountains at her back when she caught sight of movement within the bushes below. A moment later, a coyote and a badger appeared, walking side by side as they meandered through the brush.

Another odd couple, thought Blurr, remembering her first impression of Dot and Ralph.

She circled again, trying to observe these two ground hunters and what they were up to; she needed a distraction from the sadness that crept into her heart.

The coyote looked up. "Mind your own business, birdie!" he yelped.

The badger stopped short of his focused tracking of a scent and also peered upward. Blurr felt exposed now that she was noticed. She didn't fear them as long as she was up here, but she didn't want to be watched; it made her nervous.

"Come down here, little birdie," grumbled the badger. "I bet you taste sweet and juicy!"

Both the coyote and badger laughed; Blurr, on the other hand, was offended. She thought about simply leaving the two alone and moving on, but their taunting laughter was creating a surge of anger. Perhaps it was the run-in with the bat and the loss of her friends that generated a welling of frustration and anger at the world in general. She spun around and rocketed upward. Blurr topped out her ascent and let her body slow to a momentary stop. She leaned slightly, allowing her body to invert, her head facing down as she began to accelerate.

The coyote and badger lingered among the bushes, watching the falcon curiously. Their laughter stopped as they saw her power dive heading straight for them.

"*Kirrrreeeeee!*" Blurr screamed at the top of her lungs.

The coyote and badger looked at each other in bewilderment; the thought of a falcon attacking them seemed outrageous. "Let's get out of here!" whimpered the coyote; they both turned and ran, the coyote leaving the badger far behind.

Blurr was quickly approaching the ground; she pulled up at the last minute, wind rushing through her feathers. She extended her feet and flared her talons. "Do you want to eat me now?!" she yelled as she flew within inches of the badger's back. At that moment, the badger panicked and tripped on his own feet, rolling to a stop, his body consumed in flying dust.

Blurr looked back, satisfied and feeling a sense of release from pent-up anger. The coyote had disappeared into the tall bushes. *That felt good!*

She had just started to resume her flight to nowhere when a scream came from overhead.

∞

It was too late. The red-tailed hawk was upon her a second later. She instinctively rolled, talons outstretched and ready for an attack.

"Wait!" cried the hawk. "I don't want to fight you!"

The momentum of the barrel roll put Blurr right again. She screamed and rolled a second time, the hawk paralleling her flight just feet above her back. Blurr felt exposed and vulnerable.

At the second roll, the hawk blurted, "I told you I'm not here to fight!"

The hawk allowed Blurr to steady her flight and rise to the hawk's level. They flew side by side, the hawk speaking quickly, "I saw what you did to that badger," she said, her voice was clear and excited. "We need birds like you."

Blurr was absolutely confused. She knew falcons and hawks did not get along and sometimes would kill each other for territory or food. Here she was flying next to her mortal enemy; she mentally cursed herself because her first impression of this hawk was that she seemed so regal. The hawk's plumage was perfectly groomed, every feather's pattern contributed to a brilliant spectacle of whites, reds, and browns. *Stay your distance, Blurr. Be ready for an attack*, she told herself.

The hawk waited for a response; when none came, she decided to continue, "My name is Ki'ta," she said. "And my race is going to war."

∞

"Why do you need me?" Blurr asked suspiciously.

"If you put all the races of hawks together," Ki'ta said, doing much less flapping of wings than Blurr, "our numbers would still not stand a chance against our enemy."

"Who then," Blurr said, "is your enemy?"

"Demons," Ki'ta announced, her words laced in hatred. "Vile night hunters who kill everything in their path, including us!"

The birds rose higher in the air, Blurr was listening so intently she didn't realize they were equal with the peaks of mountains in the distance. "I have awoken to many a morning where we have lost family and many chicks to the demons. We try to fend them off, but we are swamped by their numbers."

Blurr thought about what she had collided with last night. "Do these 'demons,'" she asked, "look like large bats?"

At that, the hawk cackled a series of cries and looked at Blurr in surprise. "You've seen them then?" Blurr nodded and told her the story about the ambush on the cliff face and the collision and the losing of Dot and Ralph.

At the mention of befriending a vulture, Blurr noticed a repugnant look on the hawk's face.

"Then you have fought these demons," said Ki'ta, "and lived to tell about it!"

Blurr didn't really see what she did as actual fighting; it was more of a tale of getting lucky enough to run away. Ki'ta seemed to be in deep thought. "You must come with me, to my home nest!" she said suddenly.

The thought of going into an enemy's encampment surrounded by who knows how many hawks sounded like a ridiculous idea. "No, thanks," Blurr said emphatically.

"You know the enemy," Ki'ta implored. "No one has been that close and has lived to tell us about them . . . you must come!"

They had changed direction and were flying away from the large mountain range and instead were heading toward a series of rolling, tree-covered hills coated in a dull-red dust. "I must try to find my friends," Blurr retorted. She had decided she would look for them as long as she felt there was a chance they were alive.

"My family can help you," Ki'ta said earnestly. "We can send out scouts. Many eyes searching will be better than only yours."

Blurr admitted to herself that Ki'ta seemed genuine in her words; she couldn't sense deception or evil intentions. She also couldn't argue the fact that many hawks searching for her friends would be far better than she alone; she was still new to this land and wouldn't know where to start looking, except for the forest below the cliff, and she definitely didn't want to go there alone.

"All right," said Blurr with resolution, "I will go and tell your race what I saw. In return, I want help finding my friends."

The hawk bowed her head low as she soared then raised it again. "Come," she cried, "this way!"

Chapter 13

Lost Prize

Officer Perry Gomez was ending his day shift; it was the early evening in the summertime in Jackson and that meant lots of tourists. He didn't mind the busy days though–pointing people in the right direction, answering unfathomable amounts of questions of where to go see moose, bison, or bears. The onslaught of the tourist season kept his mind off Ed Riser's upcoming memorial service. He remembered the call soon after the fire was extinguished.

"Jackson 261," said the dispatch. It was Angie, and she sounded concerned over the radio.

"261," answered Perry, "go ahead."

"Fire chief will be calling you, 261," Angie said.

A moment later, Perry's cell phone rang; he pulled his police cruiser into the nearest parking lot. He had a feeling what this was about; he hoped it was going to be good news despite his suspicions.

"Perry?" said the fire chief in a grave but tender tone. "I'm sorry to say we found your friend, Ed Riser, in the cabin."

Perry listened as the fire chief recounted that Ed was found on the floor in a position that suggested he was trying to get to the back door. *Trying to save his bird I bet*, Perry thought.

It had taken a few days to make the arrangements for a service. Ed's family decided to have the service outside. They said it's what Ed would have wanted. Perry was thinking about getting a bite to eat before the service when the radio chimed in. "Dispatch!" crackled an excited voice. "We need extra units in the park, they've found something."

"Well," sighed Perry, "I'm a town cop and that's out of my jurisdiction." It was time; he called in to dispatch announcing he was going home. But first, he needed something to eat.

∞

"Chicks," crooned Dad, "you've done a great job. I'm very proud of . . . what was that?"

All three ravens jumped as voices could be heard coming from under the lowest branches of the pine tree. Dad motioned to his young to be still and quiet. They all recognized the voices as distinctly human. A giant bat swaddled in a huge bundle of pine boughs, twigs of all kinds, and a mishmash of string, old rope, and even some wire was sitting fifteen feet up from the ground, balancing precariously on a large pine branch.

"What is that?" said the park ranger to his partner.

The other ranger just stared in amazement. It looked like someone rolled up a bear-sized animal in vegetation and stuck it in a tree. "Should we try to pry it off the branch?" asked the younger ranger.

"Definitely," replied the older man. "We've got to check this out."

The two men found a long enough branch and began poking the object tenderly at first; it didn't budge. "This thing's heavier than I thought," said the older ranger.

Dad, Right, and Left stood watching as the men tried to take their prize. Frustration was mounting in the ravens; they had worked all day weaving the material to ensnare their captive. The creature almost escaped once due to the fact that they were pulling so hard. The giant wrapped figure was dislodged and fell through the pine branches landing where it sat now, in full view of people.

"I see the ravens we heard," said the younger ranger, "up in this tree. You don't think they had something to do with this?"

"Don't be silly, Justin," said the older ranger. "Ravens are smart, but with the attention span of my nephew in math class. I doubt they would have the fortitude to overcome and tie up something like this."

"So," Justin said tentatively, he didn't want to sound stupid in front of his seasoned partner, "from what I can see from here, do you think this could be what Tom saw a few weeks ago with those two ladies taking pictures?"

Scott Bloom had been a park ranger for a long time. He had seen lots of weird things before, and he was pretty sure he had seen about every kind of animal in the national park. He'd come across bears, wolves, cougars, moose, elk, bighorn sheep, pronghorn antelope, and all sorts of little creatures scampering about; but huge bats with glowing eyes and faces like a wolf? *I don't think so.*

"One more should do it," Scott said as both rangers managed to push the cocoon-like structure off the big branch. It dropped to the ground with a dull thud upon the detritus of the fallen pine needles and duff. That's when the scream filled the forest and the cocoon began to move. "We better call dispatch," Scott said as both rangers stepped back in fear.

Chapter 14

Birth of Darwin

Dr. Erin Simms was sipping tea; she was finishing some records and had just made her last call of the day to a client about a tumor found on a two-year-old Labrador.

"I'm going home, Erin," said a young girl dressed in blue scrubs as she poked her head into the doorway. "Great job today!"

"Thanks, Rachel," Erin said with a tired smile. "You too."

Erin had done four surgeries, and after an afternoon of seeing clients, she just wanted to get home and have dinner with her husband and kids. She had been married to Daniel for almost fifteen years. They lived in a nice little cabin in the woods with their two kids, Anne and Drew. Her thoughts turned to her husband. He was known to make up some crazy stories to make her laugh, but the one about giant bats and the FBI was one of the craziest, especially when he told her it was true.

"What does the FBI want with me?" Erin had asked that night, Daniel leaning against the kitchen counter. He told her that they intended on apprehending some specimens in order to figure out how to deal with them, and they needed a vet with some experience.

"I don't have experience in mutant bat medicine, Daniel," she had blurted.

"I know," Daniel had said soothingly. "But from Sherman's description, your experience in raptors and wolverines might be just what they need."

Erin had had time to think about it and process what she would be getting into. The suspense of waiting for some secret agent to call her ever floated in her mind. She wasn't supposed to tell anyone. *This was all a little crazy.*

Her cell phone buzzed in the pocket of her white coat; she pulled it out to see that it was Daniel.

"Hey, honey," Erin answered. "How was your day?"

"Hi, gorgeous," Daniel replied with hesitation. "Are you all done for the day?"

"Yeah, just have one more record to write up," Erin said.

"Great!" exclaimed Daniel, then a short pause. "Because they've got one."

Daniel pulled into the dark parking lot of the veterinary clinic. Two cars were already there, one was a Grand Teton National Park ranger's truck–the reflective green band and overhead sirens a dead giveaway even at night–the other a plain four-door sedan.

Daniel jumped out, cursing for being late. When he had gotten the call from the FBI that rangers had found a giant bat, he had been at home cooking dinner with Anne and Drew. The commute to town and then to a friend's house to drop off the kids took a while. The clinic door was ajar and a warm glow of a light was streaming out.

"What is this thing!?" Erin was saying as Daniel entered. A crowd of people were squashed into the small waiting area, everyone trying to hold down a large squirming bat bound tightly in green with an assortment of flashy colored rope the rangers had added with lots of knots. The head was covered with a bag; a muffled hiss filled the room, causing people to wince.

"It's a bat," Justin said, trying to brace himself on a lower portion of the creature. "Sort of."

"The bats I've seen," Erin said, drawing a solution into a syringe, "tend to come in smaller sizes."

Erin approached the captive cautiously; she stepped over Fitzpatrick who was splayed across the midsection like he was attempting to pin an opponent in a wrestling match. "Who's got the head of this thing?" he squeaked as he strained to keep on the massive creature.

"I got it," said Johnson who was sitting up, straddling the large head in his lap as he kept it in a headlock with his huge arms.

Daniel found a spot next to Scott Bloom and tried to put some weight on a folded wing that was spasmodically trying to extend. The wing was big and powerful, each jolt shook both he and Scott, forcing them to quickly regain balance.

"Okay, folks," Erin said, "here is to hoping I've guessed the weight on this thing. Hold on everybody!"

Erin stuck the long needle into the creature's muscle and, as quickly as she could, depressed the syringe, the liquid disappearing into the animal's body.

The creature jumped slightly, but not as much as everyone thought. Suddenly, the bat's limbs began to relax under the restraints of rope and twigs. Johnson felt the head go limp in his lap. The animal's breathing became steady and slower.

"Okay," Erin exclaimed, "let's take a look and see what we've got here."

Rangers and FBI agents began untying knots and peeling the vegetation off the beast. Erin decided to keep it on the floor in the waiting room; it was the only spot big enough to be able to spread the wings out fully.

"That's got to be at least eight feet wingspan!" Justin said amazed as Millman and Fitzpatrick held the tips of the wings, pulling them out to their full extension. Though the skin was dark, luminescent sparkles of purple shimmered under the clinic's lights.

"For a critter that would like to rip your head off," Fitzpatrick said, "it *is* kind of pretty."

"Is that a tear?" Zoe Millman said pointing with a pinky as she strained to hold the wing.

Erin Simms sidestepped over to a six-inch long rip at the trailing edge of one wing. She examined it closely, manipulating the loose flaps of skin and scraping some dried blood away. "Looks like the bleeding stopped," she said. "Not much I can do for this though unless we completely immobilize the wing."

"Hope you've got a lot of sedatives," Fitzpatrick said.

"So, Dr. Simms," Patricia Nelson said seriously, she had been relatively silent but for short commands to her agents as to where to place themselves in the restraining of the creature, "what can you tell us about this . . . animal?"

"Not much," Erin said laughing. "This is nothing like I've ever seen, it's fantastic!"

Erin probed the body, pushing in different areas, then extended the tiny legs nestled within the hairy abdomen. "What have we got here?"

"What did you find?" Daniel asked.

"Four punctures in the upper abdomen," Erin said, holding hair out of the way to get a clearer look. "Interesting arrangement of holes."

"Why do you say that, Dr. Simms?" Nelson asked curiously.

"Well," Erin said, putting her head close to the body and running a gloved finger around the rim of each wound. "I'd say that these look like holes made by talons."

"Talons of what?" Nelson pressed.

"Could be lots of things with talons this size," Erin answered, now retrieving a bottle with brown liquid sloshing inside. "Hawks and owls mostly with talons that size, maybe a large falcon. Either way, it's a nasty wound, and I need to prevent infection as much as possible."

She gave the humongous dark creature another injection and cleaned the wound with the brown solution and lots of gauze bandages.

∞

She turned to Mike Johnson, who was still refusing to let go of the head. "Well, now, that takes care of the belly, just one spot left to check." An awkward silence ensued as Mike Johnson internally deliberated as to whether to actually let go of the head. Erin approached and knelt down on both knees next to Johnson much like she had done many times for a distraught client who needed comforting. "Time to take off the hood," she said tenderly. "It will be all right."

Johnson looked perturbed that he should have to release his strangle hold; he looked at his commander for confirmation. "Go ahead," Nelson said, "but be ready for anything."

Johnson slowly released his grip enough that he could remove the hood. Everyone gasped and remained motionless. The large mouth was slightly open, revealing glistening white canines and a host of other knifelike teeth. What most kept everyone's attention, however, were the eyes. They were open and blank and were glowing blue.

"No pupil," Erin whispered, looking closer. She peered into the eye through an ophthalmoscope. She held the silver handle, shining the little light attached at the end into the blue glow.

"This is amazing," Erin yelled, completely enthralled with her exam. "No iris, no lens, in fact, I can't see any normal part of the eye at all. It's like it's just full of liquid in there."

"Great," Fitzpatrick said, still holding the wing outstretched. "Super strong, huge fangs, liquid eyes that glow in the dark, did I miss anything?"

"Yep," Zoe Millman said from the other side of the room, holding on to the other wing and smiling slightly, "a name."

Erin finished her exam of the head and was now checking the teeth. "So this is the animal Sherman thinks is millions of years old," she said, scraping plaque off a canine. "Missed out on the whole evolution thing being stuck under the ice all that time I guess?"

"We haven't determined that yet, Dr. Simms," Nelson, taking pictures with a small digital camera.

"Yeah, but," Daniel broke in, "look at it, there's no documentation of a creature like this anywhere, I've been checking. It's new . . . at least to present time."

"I understand, Mr. Simms." Nelson turned to face him. "But we still can't be sure it's some evolutionary accident and now it's going to turn everything upside down."

"I bet Charles Darwin would be turning upside down in his grave," Daniel said more to himself than anyone in particular, "if he could see this."

"That's it!" Erin blurted, smiling toward Daniel. "I think we should name him 'Darwin.'"

At that moment, the head shifted, and everybody in the room jumped. Lightning quick reflexes allowed Mike Johnson to grab the head within the crook of his arm.

"Isn't that cute?" Zoe Millman said to break the tension as everyone remained still, watching the creature intensely. "He already knows his name."

Nervous laughter echoed in the waiting room while Erin injected more anesthetic. "Given the dose I gave before," she said, pulling the needle out of the body, "this should give us enough time to get it in a cage."

Patricia Nelson put down her notepad, her heart racing after the startling move of the head. Her mind was also wheeling as to how to handle this situation. This was just one animal and it was a lot to handle, what happens when they run into more than one?

She assisted the others in getting the bat into the largest kennel they could find; with the wings bound to the body, it still filled every ounce of space. Kurt Fitzpatrick was locking the cage door looking winded when he turned to Erin who was standing beside him. "So, Doc," he said with a glimmer of a smile already growing on his face, "how do you know it's a 'him'?"

Erin smiled. "I'll let you use your imagination."

"Okay," replied Fitzpatrick sarcastically, his cowboy hat tilted and askew. "Fine, he's Darwin, but only if I can call him 'Darwin the Ferocious'!"

Chapter 15

Unlikely Friends

"I've seen your kind fly," Ki'ta commented, breaking a lasting silence between the two raptors. "You are very fast in your dives."

"Thanks," Blurr murmured. The flight had been mostly silent, both birds unsure what to say. Blurr sensed that Ki'ta was trying to make casual conversation but also felt like Ki'ta was probing her, wondering if Blurr could be trusted after all.

"My father told me that your race of falcon was the fastest flyer in the sky," Ki'ta said with just an edge of contempt. "Do you think this is true?"

Blurr sensed the challenge made by the hawk; flashes of anger prickled her muscles. She couldn't explain why she felt the need to prove herself to Ki'ta or why it angered her to be doubted of her abilities. Why was the hawk, after asking her to join the war and give her race a firsthand account of their enemy, suggest that she did not live up to a falcon's legacy?

"In the end, I think," Blurr said, concentrating on keeping calm, "we are all judged by our actions and not by the words of others."

Ki'ta smiled contentedly as if this was what she wanted to hear. "Then let's find out, shall we, falcon?"

Ki'ta led Blurr down slightly, but it wasn't but a second later that Blurr felt the warm air current pushing her upward. The hawk's broad wings caught the rising thermal easily and with little effort began to gain altitude. Blurr followed suit, though she did have to flap more often, her jet-wing-shaped wings lacking the surface area to catch the warm rising air as well as her counterpart's.

"There you go, falcon," the hawk said encouragingly. "Come touch the sun with me!"

Blurr rose still further. *I will not only touch the sun, I will fly around it!* Blurr thought as she flapped harder to keep up with Ki'ta.

"Do you like the view?" Ki'ta asked happily from just above Blurr.

Blurr had been so focused on matching the rise of Ki'ta she forgot to look down. She was higher than she had ever flown. Usually she would only go up far enough to get speed for a dive to kill her prey, but this was different. Her mind tried to calculate the distance; what few clouds there were seemed only to be specks far below her. She noticed she had a harder time breathing; the air was empty and unfulfilling.

"Get ready," Ki'ta said, looking down at her. "We're topping out."

With that, Blurr saw the rising of the hawk's body slow to almost a complete stop, like time had frozen her in midmotion. A moment passed and the dark wings retracted partway as Ki'ta let out a long shriek. Blurr watched Ki'ta's body pick up speed, and in a flash, the hawk was nothing but a black dot racing to the earth.

Blurr's mind had cleared with the anticipation of what was to come; a wisp of breeze caressed her feathers as she too paused at the top of her ascent. She tracked Ki'ta's dive; her hunting instinct kicked in. The wings folded tightly against her sides, feet snug close, and body rigid. Like a roller coaster gaining momentum, she plunged after the hawk.

There was so much free fall, her body was full of vitality and she wanted to be in this moment forever.

Ki'ta was no longer just a point of dark in the sky; Blurr was gaining quickly. She could now see the finer features of the hawk's feathers being pummeled by the dive. Blurr's sleek body pierced the air with little resistance; she was nearly even with Ki'ta. A look of surprise sprang across Ki'ta's face as Blurr whooshed past her.

Trees were rapidly approaching, Blurr was sure she had gone faster than she had ever gone before and was now concerned with pulling up. Ki'ta was somewhere behind her now; she had proven her abilities and felt that she had lived up to her falcon race.

The air was loudly pounding in her ears with turbulence. She extended her wings gradually, feeling them catch and drag her up. She had to put all her effort into holding the position until the turbulence ebbed. Her body was beginning to give under the strain of pulling out of this epic dive.

"That was amazing!" Ki'ta exclaimed when it was over and they had leveled out. "I've never seen any bird equal your speed."

"Thanks," Blurr huffed. She was feeling winded after her major recovery from the dive. "I've never been that high before."

"That's where I go to think and be alone," Ki'ta said wistfully. "These days, I spend much time aloft trying to think of a way to combat our enemy."

The birds were flying low over the tops of a stand of cottonwood trees when Blurr thought of something. "Are you a leader in your clan?"

Ki'ta was silent, as if she were choosing her words carefully. "I am . . . in a manner of speaking."

"I don't understand," Blurr said.

"I mean," Ki'ta began, "I am a leader within our race, my mother was officially our clan's *rital*, that means 'final word' in hawkish."

"Hawks have their own language?" asked Blurr. It never occurred to her that a hawk, who is such a close cousin of a falcon, would not speak her language.

"Hawks, eagles, owls, vultures," said Ki'ta offhandedly, "and even falcons, they all have their special speech. It's just that the common tongue is used most often between different races."

"I haven't spent much time with anyone but Dot and Ralph," Blurr said, "and they only seemed to speak the common tongue when I was with them."

Ki'ta looked perplexed. "How is it that you don't know such things as this?"

Blurr decided to tell Ki'ta her story of captivity, her freedom, and what had happened since. Ki'ta's reaction was that of astonishment and sadness. "How could one spend time in a cage?!" she blurted when Blurr was done.

The cottonwoods were fading and giving way to a vast expanse of green grass. Blurr saw that this grass had the signs of being managed by humans. It was lush and almost unnaturally green in such a dry area. There was a white wooden fence surrounding most of it, and there in the distance, she could see cows sprinkled here and there. She felt wary, being so close to the race of her former master made her nervous and edgy. She was now dealing with resentment toward her human master while trying to block the memories of being caged from surfacing in her mind.

The scene didn't seem to bother Ki'ta at all. The hawk casually flew at Blurr's wingtip, looking from side to side as if sightseeing on vacation. Suddenly, she turned to Blurr. "Are you hungry?"

Blurr had to think of the last time she had eaten anything. So much had happened and now at the thought of eating, she realized she was famished. She nodded eagerly.

"Look down there," Ki'ta said excitedly. Blurr scanned the area below. Just beyond the green pasture was a small pond glittering golden in the sunlight. A moment later, she found what the hawk must have been referring to, a gaggle of geese listlessly swimming at the pond's edge. They were Canada Geese, black and white patches showing easily from a distance. The large birds were enjoying the cool eddies of water on this hot afternoon.

"Have you ever hunted geese?" Ki'ta asked with anticipation.

"No," Blurr stated plainly, "they're a bit big for me."

"True," Ki'ta said, nodding. "They are big but are also very tasty. You just have to be careful as they are extremely foul tempered and can knock you senseless if given the chance."

"And you're telling me this because . . . ?" Blurr let the question hang.

"Because, dear falcon," Ki'ta replied with a gleam in her eye, "we're going to have one for lunch!"

"Oh really," Blurr said as if she couldn't believe what she heard. "And how are we supposed to kill a bird that outweighs us by . . . by a lot?"

They wheeled around the pasture; Blurr could see that Ki'ta was positioning them so that their backs were facing the sun. "I've got a plan," Ki'ta said. "But just do us both a favor–don't miss."

They flew high enough that their presence seemed to go undetected as each goose lazily floated unperturbed below. "Aren't you a bird hunter?" Ki'ta asked. When Blurr nodded she continued in a hurried voice, "If I flush them into flight, you can knock one senseless enough and I'll finish the job."

"I don't know, they're big birds–"

"They're not as big as a demon!" Ki'ta said critically, "And virtually defenseless when airborne."

"Yeah, but I wasn't really trying to hit a demon!" Blurr hissed in an undertone. Ki'ta didn't hear her; the hawk's piercing amber eyes waited for a reply, when none came, she assumed the plan was a go. Ki'ta peeled off and dove in a long arch toward the pond. Blurr could see that she was attempting to herd the geese in Blurr's direction. With the sun at Blurr's back, the geese wouldn't see her attack until it was too late.

At the first sight of the hawk, the geese began to squawk loudly in protest to the interruption of their carefree afternoon. Ki'ta swooped in, barely missing the floundering wings and extended necks of the geese trying to nip at their attacker. After several dive bombs, the geese began their departure. As if they had all decided together, each bird began to flap hard, pounding the water with each downward stroke moving into formation while their webbed feet ran on the surface of the water. Rings on the water sprang from each footfall until the birds gained enough lift to get them high enough to clear the pond's edge and surrounding plant life. One goose barely made it over a nearby fence and had to hurry to catch up.

"So that is the one she wants, huh?" Blurr said to herself as she saw Ki'ta pursue the stray goose, leaving the others to continue unmolested. Ki'ta weaved side to side, shepherding the lone goose directly under Blurr who was poised high in the sky, ready for her dive.

The moment came; the familiar rush of wind swept over her body as she careened straight toward the goose. The goose's body was rapidly approaching; she saw the back, a nice rivulet in the feathers running down the midsection denoting the spinal cord. She flared her tail a brief moment to steady herself then tucked her feet, pulled in her wings, and slammed into the back of the goose.

Smack! The impact sent Blurr off to one side. She felt bones snapping the moment she slammed into the goose's back. It was over. *There will be nothing for the hawk to finish,* thought Blurr. Though she felt a little dizzy, the soft goose was easier to hit being so large and was much softer than ducks or pigeons. She flared her tail and wings to steady her flight and made a quick turn to track the falling goose.

"I told you it would work," Ki'ta said, swooping in line with Blurr.

"Somehow," Blurr said, "I think I got the harder of the two jobs."

Ki'ta laughed a melodic, high-noted giggle. Blurr had never heard a bird laugh before. "Of course you did," Ki'ta said, "you're the *bird* hunter, remember?"

Both birds feasted on the goose until they were bloated, their crops bulging like the belly of a snake that had just swallowed an egg. Now that they were full and sitting on a branch in the shade of the afternoon sun, Blurr wanted some answers. "Ki'ta," Blurr said, breaking the silence, "you said that your mother was the *rital*, what happened to your mother?"

At this, Ki'ta, who was perching comfortably next to Blurr, fidgeted as a gloom passed over her face. Blurr regretted asking the question, breaking the mood of a good hunt and a nice meal.

"Both my mother and father were taken by demons," Ki'ta said simply.

"I'm sorry," Blurr whispered.

"It was not long after they first started hunting us," Ki'ta continued, "it has only been a little while and so many of us have been lost. We heard the bleating of chicks one night, my mother left the nest first. I could hear a great battle and could only see shadows. My father left to join her. They never came back." Ki'ta roused her feathers then settled them back into place, looking off into the distance.

"I think there is a *rital* within the demons," Ki'ta said seriously.

"You mean, one that commands them?" Blurr asked.

"Yes, but the *rital* of the demons is not like the others, she is different," Ki'ta said, her voice trailing off. "I have seen her do things . . ." Ki'ta shook as if she were trying to physically get the image out of her head.

The afternoon sun was dipping toward the mountain peaks in the distance. They were miles from the mountain range, deep within tree-covered hills. "It will be getting dark soon, we should go," Ki'ta said suddenly. Blurr got the feeling Ki'ta was not willing to answer any more questions; she nodded and they both lit from the branch.

Chapter 16

It's Just a Scratch

Sherman Hinkley was lying in his hospital bed watching television. The game was on and he needed something to take his mind of his wounds; they were inflamed and stung with pain. "But they're just scratches!" Sherman blasted at the nurses who were attending to him. *Or they could be bites*, he thought. Nevertheless, they should be healing by now.

He could tell the doctors and nurses were thinking the same thing: why weren't they healing? The skin around each cut was growing darker with weblike veins running out in all directions. Sherman thought it would look like a cool tattoo if it didn't hurt so much.

A knock came at the door. "Hello, Mr. Hinkley, can I come in?" asked the nurse.

"Yes," he replied. "I'm decent . . . enough."

The nurse entered. She was wearing teal-colored scrubs and well-worn sandals; her red hair was pinned back in a bun. "How are you feeling tonight?"

"Like crap," Sherman said grouchily.

The nurse simply smiled. She was used to grumpy patients, she had developed a "sunshine smile" as she called it, to display at times like these. "It's time for our shift change, Mr. Hinkley, Susan will be taking my place for the night. Do you remember her?"

Susan was about four feet high and the same width and reminded Sherman of his uncle Charlie. She even had a mustache. "Yes, I remember her," he said plainly.

"Good. Just remember to get some rest tonight, Mr. Hinkley," she said kindly. "Remember, the doctors are going to be reassessing your . . . condition tomorrow."

Sherman gave her a thin smile as she left his room. *Yeah, reassess and ship me off to Salt Lake City to some specialist.* He knew if the doctors here can't figure something out, patients get turfed to Salt Lake City, the nearest and biggest resource of medical help.

Sherman continued to watch the game. He felt drowsy and lost track of time, every once in a while he would awake to cheering from the television as someone had scored but would quickly drift into a restless slumber. He awoke suddenly, not to cheering this time but to an intense pain in his legs. He sat bolt upright as if stung into wakefulness, the burning sensation crept like wildfire up his legs. He gritted his teeth and whipped the sheets off to reveal his bare legs. To his horror, he saw that they had shrunken as if they were dehydrated like beef jerky. His feet were not human, but instead had three long frail toes with a claw at each end. He twisted his body to reach for the "call" button, only to find that his arms were numb with pain; he couldn't move them.

He tried to scream but only yielded clicks as his flesh boiled like he had put his entire face into a scalding pot of oil and began to balloon out into a doglike snout with long white fangs bursting through his gums. He writhed in pain and knocked over a dinner tray as his arms expanded into giant membranous wings almost touching the walls on either side of his room.

Sherman peered around the room, his neck felt loose and as flexible as a rubber band as it swiveled from side to side in blind confusion. The room's lights were so bright it was painful, like megawatt beams burning into his eye sockets; he knew he must find darkness. He moved, his bat-like body was clumsy and awkward as he fell to the floor. He extended a wing with great effort and soreness and managed to click the lights off. The television coated the room in flickering lights; it was the only source of light now, and the pain in his eyes was more tolerable. His thin translucent ears jerked rapidly from side to side, tracking every sound wave flowing through the room, the sports announcer's voice pierced his mind like a spear, loud and thunderous. Without thinking, he envisioned a cloudy film fill his mind, muffling the sound of the television. Sherman drew a long breath as his mind relaxed a moment while he sat in the corner of his room on the cold tile floor. He closed his eyes, too afraid to open them for fear that everything he had just endured was real and that this wasn't some twisted nightmare. He saw himself lying in his hospital bed, whole and fully a person. He inhaled deeply one more time and opened his eyes.

Sherman smelled something akin to a wet dog and realized it was his new body. He crinkled his nose and felt the lips curl back. He delicately slid his tongue along the exposed fangs feeling every indention and point. His eyes roved from one side to the other, he scanned his thin membranous wings hanging limply to his sides. He pulled them in self consciously and tucked them closed to his hairy mid-section. The room's details were vivid even in the dwindling light, for a moment he took wonder in this; focusing on every etch in wood, every glimmer of chrome, every fold in linens. His brief reprieve of introducing himself to his new skills was cut abruptly with a voice in the hallway.

His ears twitched for a fix on waves of vibrations pushing their way through his mind. He marveled at the fact that the sound waves returning to his senses created a picture of a human in his mind. By the dimensions, Sherman guessed it was Nurse Susan.

"I'll be there in a minute," Susan said just outside the closed door. "I just want to check on captain grumps, I thought I heard something."

Sherman heard everything as if Susan was whispering in his ear in a quiet room, yet she was outside in the corridor. The words came to him like smoke with texture that he could read and understand. Sherman blinked two huge glowing blue eyes in shock as several random images that were not his own, formed in his mind. The first was an impression of a list of groceries bought that day, but something was forgotten; then relief at opening an envelope with a check made out to Susan Riddick; and finally a large donut which was accompanied by lots of anticipation. Sherman realized in shock that he was listening to her thoughts.

The doorknob jostled. Sherman scanned the room for a way to escape; the window was shut and locked, with his new limbs he thought it would be futile to try to manipulate the levers and go through the window. The door was his only option. He pried himself into a somewhat stable pushup position, his wings bent and acting like braces on the slippery linoleum. He knew any moment the nurse was going to enter the room, see him crouched in the corner and go hysterically running for help. His mind flashed with images of his new body riddled with tranquilizer darts as scientists leered over him ready to find out what made him tick. He knew he had to get away from here, had to get away from people.

He wobbled forward and crouched on the floor behind the bed feeling his strange new body struggling simply to keep him upright. Light pierced the darkened room in an even ray through the crack created as the door opened slightly. Nurse Susan, noticing that only the television was on, whispered softly, "Good evening, Mr. Hinkley. It's Susan, just wanted to check on you."

When there wasn't an answer, Nurse Susan pushed the door open more, her wide frame blocking most of the light from the corridor. Sherman was squashed against the far corner, one more step and she would see him. He thought about busting the window, but it was a two-paned glass and thick enough to avoid letting in cold air during the long winters, he wasn't sure he could even crack it with his new body.

Sherman realized that the pain was gone. His transformation was complete and his mind was clear, clearer than it ever had been in his whole life.

He sensed many minds within the hospital besides Susan's, though the other thought patterns were detected only by vague echoes of human consciousness that Sherman could not decipher. Nurse Susan's thoughts on the other hand were registering clearly like dead-on radio reception. He could hear her thoughts about how she was longing to be done with this shift because she was getting sick and just wanted to go home. Sherman closed his glowing eyes and focused his concentration on the nurse. He felt the sensation of drifting through mists and vortexes of sounds and feelings until he knew that he had come to a barrier that was the entry point to Nurse Susan's mind. He didn't know how he knew it was hers, he just knew.

He concentrated until he could feel his conscious self push through the barrier. It was like trying to pull through a slimy mud wall; cold and oppressive. He continued to push through the darkness and dampness until his sight became clear. His conscious awareness was flooded by dazzling images that revolved around him in a swirling stream of colors and images like thousands of home movies playing in the same theatre at once. Sherman peered around the mind of Nurse Susan, feeling like he was in a pinball machine as brilliant images of color and feelings whipped past him in random directions. He saw fleeting visuals of Susan's memories from as recent as moments ago when she clicked her time card into the machine on the wall to random flashbacks of her ten year old self being pelted by snowballs as a child and crying.

Sherman was mesmerized at first, like walking into a disco and being entranced by the spinning ball and glittering lights. Then just as quickly something deeper in his consciousness alerted him to the need for action to facilitate his escape. He saw the time card memory whip past him again and suddenly had an idea. His amorphous self calmed and refocused its attention on the swirling images running helter skelter around him. He visualized a time card that never passed through the machine on the wall and inserted a large dose of worry about payment for lost time on the job. He let the thought trail from his conscious self and weave its way into the fray of frenetic thought patterns.

Sherman's consciousness laughed in spite of itself, the idea of entering another's mind would have been a ridiculous notion to consider hours ago and here he was, probing the mind of a stranger with relative ease, despite the nasty entry through the cold and slimy wall. He even chuckled at the audacity to try to insert his own thought pattern into her mind in an attempt to influence it to his own personal gain. He felt like a computer virus, only he was living and aware of everything he was doing. He just didn't know if it was going to work.

Suddenly Susan stopped dead in her tracks, closed the door and walked briskly back down the corridor.

Sherman's consciousness was immediately yanked from her mind, passing through the cold wall like being drug by a towrope attached to an airplane. A wave of nausea hit him and he crouched even lower to the ground like a dog ready to vomit. He froze, waiting for the feeling to pass and it did as quickly as it came. He was alone and suddenly very pleased with himself. He felt powerful.

Sherman sat alone in the dark room. It took him several tries, but he eventually hit the power button to the television set with a small claw that hung on the bend of the leading edge of his wing. He needed quiet to think of a plan to get out of this building. He had to get out of here, but he knew somehow that he would not be able to take all the lighting in the hallway, not to mention running into the night-shift staff.

His mind raced; he couldn't be seen. He knew large dangerous-looking animals among people meant lots of guns and his head mounted on somebody's wall. Quick visions of his wolf-bat head decorating a hunting lodge loomed in his mind. Suddenly, he had an idea. He closed his eyes and reached out to the nearest mind he could latch on to, passing through the cold wall, though this time it was thinner. He wasn't sure, but he sensed it was the tall man that sat at the desk three doors down the corridor. He inserted a thought pattern like before, letting it snake into the meandering mind of his host. He backed out on his own this time, returning to his own self. He was getting the hang of this, he thought.

Sherman waited patiently for only a few moments when he noticed through the space between the door and the floor that the lights in the corridor flickered then went out. He smiled, or thought he was smiling. He couldn't really tell with his new long snout and a mouth full of teeth.

Sherman guessed he was about the size of a Collie with at least eight feet of wingspan. From this new perspective, the doorknob was much higher than he realized, and without opposable thumbs, it was going to be a challenge. He remembered an old college buddy who had trained his Border Collie to fetch a beer from the refrigerator, he clutched the slippery steel knob with his jaws and twisted. After three tries he managed to twist the doorknob enough to unlatch it. He pulled the door open enough to let go and jam his head in the opening. He winced in pain as the door wedged his head tightly against the threshold. He mentally cursed the strength of the self closing mechanism at the top of the door. Sherman's bat body was very pliable, and he began to easily squeeze through the opening, first a wing, then his body, then retracting the other wing through the space, his head attempting to twist with his body but still wedging the door. *If momma could see me now*, he thought as he felt his neck morbidly twisting with his body movement. He now appreciated the long flexible necks of swans as they preened their backsides. He pulled his head back in relief, letting the door close quietly. His eyes could see every detail of everything as if the lights were still on, only anything that was living seemed to exude a glow that enveloped the bodies of the people like an aura. The slippery tiled floors were hard to maneuver upon, but eventually, he got into a rhythm and was nearly at the emergency exit just around the corner when his satellite-shaped ears twitched. He sensed many minds racing down hallways in several directions. Controlling the mind of the attendant at the desk to trip the circuit breaker was now causing the predictable havoc–just what he needed.

Sherman leaned on the emergency handle of the door and pushed with all his strength. A loud bell rang; he would only have seconds to get out before crowds of people showed. Again he squeezed through using a similar technique as before. At last, he was outside; the night was cool and inviting. He could see the extreme details of objects as well as a host of nighttime insects that he thought would go completely undetected if he still had his human eyesight.

He looked up at the stars and extended his wings out to both sides. He would have to let this amazing and life-changing event process later; right now, he needed to attempt to fly.

Chapter 17

Darwin's Awakening

Darwin woke up with a pounding headache. When he opened his eyes, everything was blurry, and he felt cold. His body trembled and shook every time he took a breath. His mind was blank; usually it was filled with the thoughts of his queen. His desire to obey her was all he knew. He felt alone and disconnected from his family, empty, and hollow. He rotated his ears to sweep the surroundings for incoming signals telling him where his queen was. There was nothing.

He sent clicks of signals of his own, calling for his family to find him; there was no reply. He swelled with sadness and despair; he felt vulnerable and dead and wished he could really die at this moment. To be disconnected from his family and his queen was unbearable; they were always connected, always communicating their thoughts and feelings. Being alone was never an option; his thoughts were given to him by his queen. *She was always right.*

The silence was broken by the opening of a door. "I just want to check on him one more time," Erin said as she exited the back door. The air was frigid, and she could see her breath.

Darwin could see the face clearly through the cage door; she peered through the slats. "Hi, Darwin," she said, "I imagine you're feeling woozy, but that will fade and hopefully you'll feel better in the morning."

Woozy? Better? His mind processed the words and seemed to understand them. He could feel her sympathy and know she meant well but was cautious of him.

He was dizzy with his own thoughts swirling around in his mind. He was used to commands, direct and without question. This freedom of mind was uncomfortable, and he felt like his balance was challenged at every step.

"Well," Erin said, shining a small light into his face and down to his belly, "your wounds are healing amazingly fast. It's only been a few hours since you got here."

He could understand her. He knew what she was saying, but how?

His queen was not sending him signals, translating for him. He could not feel her presence and mentally groped for direction from her; the blank void of silence in his mind encroached upon him. "I'm sorry to leave you alone overnight," Erin said regretfully, "but this is a small clinic and the FBI folks don't want anyone else to know about you. I'm coming first thing in the morning though, okay?"

I am scared, he thought as he understood her to be leaving him.

The thought hung in his mind. Floods of fear welled within him; he could not remember ever feeling such a thing. The face of the stranger peering at him became intense.

"I know you're scared," Erin said blankly, as if she couldn't decide if she really knew what the animal was feeling. "I will help you, okay?"

Darwin felt comforted by this odd being. Her words, or rather her thoughts, were genuine and true. *Thank you.*

Erin reeled back; she fumbled for something to sit on, finally placing herself on a nearby empty kennel. Her face was white, the powerful image of gratitude was unmistakable, and it blanketed her mind. She looked at the beast and focused her own thoughts this time. *Nod your head if you can hear me*, she thought. Erin felt like she was going crazy until she witnessed the gigantic head of the bat nod his head slowly.

Oh God, Erin thought. She stood up with complete resolution and said, "I've got to get you out of here."

Darwin felt his body, still bound by bandages with his wings tightly tied to his frame, jostled as Erin pushed the cage to her truck. It took many attempts, but eventually, Erin succeeded in getting Darwin's cage into her pickup truck. She sped home, still not sure how she was going to explain this to Daniel who would be putting the kids to bed right about now.

"This is crazy, Erin," she said to herself as she drove along the highway. "I must be out of my mind!"

When she pulled into the driveway, she could see only the upstairs bedroom light on. *Thank goodness, the kids are asleep and Daniel is waiting for me,* she thought, taking a breath. She parked the truck, got out, and rounded to the cage stuffed in the back. "You stay here, okay? You'll be safe here, understand?" Erin said louder than she intended, holding her hands outward.

Again, to her amazement, the animal nodded. Erin smiled and sprang to the house. She was going to have to word her explanation in just the right way or Daniel would freak at her seemingly impulsive decision. Before going to the front door, she stopped and closed her eyes, focusing a clear thought in her mind, *I am Erin.*

She waited excitedly, hoping her hunch was right. The darkness was absolute; only the stars broke the night sky, but she could still see her breath. She waited only a moment when a distinct thought entered her head like a polite guest into her home, *I am Darwin.*

Giddy, Erin opened the door and entered the house; she decided there was only one way to convince Daniel of what she discovered.

Darwin waited, bound and in darkness. Without his queen to guide his thoughts, the stranger's mind was the only thing he felt that was comforting. He longed for her to return, to give him solace and assurance that all would be well, when suddenly, his ears twitched with signals coming from nearby.

"You step on my foot one more time, Ralph!" squeaked the first voice, sounding very annoyed.

"Sorry," came the reply, "there's not much room on this branch!"

"Well, since I can see at night, I can tell you that there is plenty of room on *that* branch!"

"Then I will go to *that* branch, fine with you?"

"Fine with me!"

"Dot?"

"Yeah."

"Where is *that* branch?"

Darwin could hear the noises, but it was the thoughts that he could understand. He sat perched at the back of the cage, a wide bandage around his body; he hopped to the front gate and peered in the direction of the signals.

Are you my enemy? Darwin thought.

"Did you hear that, Ralph?" Dot said from the top of a tree branch. Both he and Ralph had been resting for the night in a nice-looking pine tree when they were disturbed by bright lights from the truck.

"Nope," Ralph said calmly. "Hear what?"

"Must be nothing," Dot said dismissively.

Darwin followed the conversation; he could understand every word, though he didn't know how or why; he repeated the thought signal. Instantly, Dot squeaked and fluttered his wings as if he was being swarmed by mosquitos.

"What's wrong, Dot?" Ralph said concerned.

"You're telling me you don't hear that?!" Dot blurted, huffing.

Ralph looked perplexed. Dot was scanning the nighttime landscape; only the house and the truck were visible for the most part. He couldn't understand why his mind was being invaded by this question: *Are you my enemy?*

Just then, the driveway lit up by a light pouring out from the front door of the house. "Just hear me out, okay?" Erin was saying as she led Daniel to the back of the truck.

"You brought it here?" Daniel exclaimed alarmingly.

"Wait!" Erin said. She faced Darwin, now at the front of the cage looking like a convict strapped in a straight jacket. "Darwin," she said slowly, "nod your head if you can understand me."

"Look, Erin," Daniel started, "I know you want to help this animal but . . ."

Daniel stopped talking as if someone had pressed a "pause" button. He stood motionless, eyes fixed on the animal in the cage that just nodded its head slowly. Erin watched and smiled eagerly. "So?" she asked.

Daniel looked at Erin in astonishment. "You're Doctor Dolittle.," he said blankly.

"I know, right?" Erin said happily, "Wait, there's more, I'm going to think something to him and ask him to respond to both of us."

"He can do that?" Daniel blurted.

"He thought to me earlier, but I'm willing to bet he can do the same to you, too."

"I don't know Erin," Daniel cautioned taking a small step backward, "this is freaking me out enough without this thing wandering around in my head too."

"Just trust me Daniel," Erin soothed but was shaking with anticipation, "I don't know how, but I feel that we can trust him."

"Okay," Daniel mumbled, "but start small, nothing . . . you know, complicated."

Erin smiled and closed her eyes. "Wait!" Daniel exclaimed, "How will I know if he's answering your question or I'm just imagining him talking to me? Maybe you better whisper the question in my ear first."

Erin relented and leaned over to his ear. A moment later she regained her composure and began to focus once more.

"Yeah," Daniel said nodding, "that is a good question."

Several moments passed in silence, only the cool night breeze blowing nearby branches softly could be heard. Daniel waited, feelings of doubt and a little disappointment crept into his mind. There was a part of him that wanted to be telepathically talked to by this strange creature. He slumped his shoulders disappointedly and was about to say something when his mind was flooded with images and words.

Erin watched Daniel's face turn ashen white with a vacant stare, his eyes fixed on some distant point, his breathing shallow. She smiled, she had just received the signal too, though for some reason it didn't affect her in the same way as Daniel.

"Honey?" Erin whispered, "Are you okay?"

Daniel nodded, still dazed. "We're going to have to tell those FBI agents what he just told us, aren't we?"

"Yep." Erin replied quietly.

"They're not going to like it one bit," Daniel said still staring at the hunched creature in the darkened cage."

Erin and Daniel stood in shock next to the cage, the light from the house casting long shadows down the driveway.

∞

With each passing minute, Darwin was feeling more and more liberated in thought and feeling. The disconnection from his queen had opened a floodgate of ideas and ambitions. He never felt so alive and eager to explore and learn. It was all coming so fast; he didn't know how to respond and was a little thankful for being locked in a cage where he could process this transformation.

I have been a slave, he thought in disgust, *a slave in both mind and body.*

"How long before he can fly?" Daniel asked suddenly.

Erin thought a moment. "He's healing remarkably fast, maybe by tomorrow."

"We have a living organism that is not human, and yet we can communicate with it on a complex level–with thoughts alone," Daniel said in complete amazement.

"I know!" Erin said. "What are we going to do, if they keep Darwin, he'll be locked up in high security somewhere and poked and prodded, we can't give him over to the Feds!"

The cage rattled as Darwin lurched at Erin's words. She quickly touched the cage. "Don't worry, Darwin, we'll keep you safe."

Darwin settled but could feel her anxiousness and absorbed her worry. He could feel the same from the male, though his was much a simpler feeling, more primitive but still genuine. He knew he could trust the animal called Erin most of all.

"Okay," Daniel said, "we've got to think and make a list of options. We'll be back, Darwin!"

Both Erin and Daniel fled inside, leaving Darwin to contemplate his predicament when he detected the two eavesdroppers from above. Both were observing the conversation, but they did not understand what was said. *However, they could help me*, he thought.

Darwin sent a signal requesting the aid of these two life forms from the nearest tree. He received initial resistance from the smaller of the two, but eventually they complied. A moment later two shapes landed on the ground in front of his cage. A large black bird with a wrinkly pink head stood nervously in the driveway tapping one foot on the gravel. Next to him was a tiny owl with large yellow eyes, ruffled feathers, and a very perturbed look about him. They both stood side by side looking transfixed as they stared into Darwin's two eerie, glowing eyes.

Darwin realized that there was little time left; he needed to confront his queen and he needed to get out of this cage . . . now!

Chapter 18

Rodeo Sighting

Patricia Nelson sat on the edge of her hotel room bed, reading the local newspaper feeling frustrated. The headline read, "More Sightings of Valley Monster!" She read about how two more children had been taken and law enforcement was coming up empty. "We are not commenting on this investigation at this time," a detective was quoted. "We are still following several leads and are very hopeful."

"Yeah," Nelson said, "that's cop talk for 'we have jack squat.'" She set the paper down and sighed. At least a little good news was that the people who saw the creature they had captured tonight were keeping quiet, at least for now. That was something.

"Howdy, Patricia!" Kurt Fitzpatrick said, smiling as he strolled in the open doorway. He was wearing brand new Wrangler jeans, shiny brown cowboy boots that were silver tipped at the toe, and his big black cowboy hat. "Guess what?" he said enthusiastically. "They're having a rodeo tonight, right here in town!"

"You're kidding," Nelson said. "You want to go to this thing?"

He threw the brochure on the bed then sat down in a nearby chair, still smiling. Nelson noticed that Kurt wasn't shaving as much lately and getting scruffy looking.

"So?" Fitzpatrick asked like a child waiting to see if it was okay for him to go out and play.

"How is going to a rodeo going to help us in our mission, Kurt?" Nelson asked point-blank.

Fitzpatrick's shoulders slumped slightly. After a moment's pause, he smiled again. "You know," he began, "there are lots of people at these rodeos

I hear, lots of locals too. We could take the opportunity to get information from them, see if anyone has seen anything unusual."

Nelson couldn't think of a retort. "Okay," she said slowly, "but I expect you to be questioning a lot of people and not just watching the bullfights!"

"Of course," he responded, straining to control his excitement, then he leaned closer to her. "You mean bull riders."

"Whatever."

A vibration at her hip told Patricia Nelson that she had a message on her BlackBerry. She whipped it off her belt fluidly. "Looks like Johnson and Millman are on their way back."

"Did they remember the peanut butter?" Fitzpatrick asked. After the ordeal at the veterinary clinic, they were tired and wanted to debrief the next step over whatever Millman and Johnson picked up at the grocery store. Nelson raised an eyebrow. "Didn't say, but said that we'll like it."

Minutes later, the door opened. "Can you believe they have sushi here!?" Zoe Millman yelled in excitement as she entered the hotel room carrying a bag of groceries. Mike Johnson followed closely behind her with a stern face carrying a huge bag that bulged on all sides and a large tray of sushi covered in plastic wrap.

"Room service!" Fitzpatrick said, taking the sushi tray from Johnson. "Thank you, I love this stuff!"

Kurt Fitzpatrick explained to Millman and Johnson that they were going to a rodeo to do some questioning of the local townsfolk. Millman sat down at the small round table looking happily at the array of multicolored sushi rolls lying in perfect rows on the tray, "What do you expect to find there?" she said grabbing a roll with small orange bead-like eggs on the top, "'Oh yeah, I know exactly where the bat things are and the missing kids, but I just wanted to watch some guy break his nose riding a cow first'?" The petite agent stuffed the sushi roll into her mouth. She was by far the smallest in size but had the biggest appetite of them all. Even Johnson couldn't seem to devour as much food as she could.

"Look," Fitzpatrick pleaded, "I know we have one of those things in custody, but there are more out there and kids are disappearing. So I thought why not go to a big town event, full of people that live all over the county, and ask what they've seen!" Fitzpatrick waited as everyone simply stared at him. "It can't hurt, can it?"

∞

They reached the rodeo grounds sooner than they thought. Walking only a few blocks of residential streets, they could hear the crowd cheering.

The voice of the announcer filled the air, a man in an elevated box peered out of a slide window holding a microphone. "Ladies and gentlemen, that there is two thousand pounds of frustrated farm animal."

The crowd laughed and the four FBI agents entered via a ticket booth, each getting a stamp on their hand. "It's a smiley face," Fitzpatrick said, looking at the back of his hand. Three of the agents were dressed in jeans and collared shirts. Fitzpatrick, however, was strutting in his full Western garb; Nelson thought she noticed him tipping his hat to a couple of young girls as he passed. She rolled her eyes.

"There are some empty seats up there," Millman said, pointing to the top row of a set of bleachers. The area was lit up like a football stadium, with bleachers found on all sides, but only one side had a giant awning that covered everyone down to the first row. They walked through the crowds of people standing in lines to get beer and nachos at the snack stands and then climbed the stairs to the top row of bleachers.

There were several people in the arena, one of which had a headset and was dressed in baggy overalls and bright yellow and red socks. He strode about the arena cracking jokes while the riders were getting ready. Speakers rang out over the crowd, "This next bull is as fierce as a rattlesnake and dang near as ugly as my Aunt Marty!"

"People want to do this?" Millman asked as the crowd screamed; a giant black bull burst from the pen while the speakers blasted AC/DC's *Back in Black*. The rider bounced with every bone-jarring motion, his arms and legs flapping wildly like a rag doll in the hands of a two-year-old throwing a tantrum. Seconds later, the cowboy launched himself off the bovine still bucking and thrashing its horns in every direction. Nelson could hear the crowd groan in vicarious pain when the rider landed in a jumbled heap of limbs on the sandy ground. A moment went by in hushed silence as everyone waited for the cowboy to move. Meanwhile, three riders on horseback directed the bull away from the cowboy and into the pen. However, the bull refused to go.

"Looks like our bull, Picante, doesn't want to go home," the announcer said. "Maybe our bullfighters can help."

"See!" Nelson exclaimed. "They do have bullfighters here."

"Okay," Fitzpatrick said quickly, "but they're dressed like clowns."

Suddenly, the DJ put theme music from *Jaws* through the system, which echoed around the arena. As if on cue, the bull lowered his horns and pawed the ground. One bullfighter jumped into a hollow barrel while the other threw it on one side and rolled it tauntingly toward the bull. The slow pulsating beat of the music quickened as the bullfighter rolled the barrel with the other bullfighter inside within inches of the lowered head. The crowd was silent as well as the announcer.

The huge animal lunged and raked the barrel, propelling it into the air; the other bullfighter scurried to the side waving his hands and the bull redirected his attention on the man. Suddenly, three riders on horseback entered the fray in beautiful symmetry. The bull stepped back and regressed back in to the pen. The gate closed and the crowd went wild with applause.

"Tim Walters finished with a qualifying time," said the announcer in the box. "Give it up for that brave cowboy, not everyone can ride a bull that looks like his Aunt Marty!"

The crowd roared, applauded, and giggled as the bullfighter who was thrown in the barrel popped out and said through his portable microphone, "Anyone see my teeth?"

Nelson was absolutely speechless. She couldn't understand why anyone would put themselves through that much punishment. She was sure that those young men were going to have huge orthopedic bills later in life. They watched several bull riders, bronc riders, and even some team roping. The night had cooled off considerably, and she shivered slightly. She needed to stretch and move; they had been sitting on the hard bleachers for almost an hour. "I'm going to walk around, maybe talk to some people," she said to the others.

Instantly, Fitzpatrick shot up as if to come along. She motioned for him to sit. "Enjoy yourself, this city girl has had enough." The agent sat back down slowly, but she could tell he was glad to stay.

Patricia Nelson sauntered through the rodeo grounds, lingering by lines of people and eavesdropping on as many conversations as possible. She really didn't know where to start and she thought this was quite a fruitless activity. She had decided the likelihood of getting any viable information about anything other than horses or truck tires was unlikely. She found herself under a section of bleachers; thick stripes of shadows blanketed the ground. She moved through the supportive poles not really looking for anything in particular when she heard someone say "bat" right above her.

Patricia Nelson went tense and into FBI mode; her mind became acute, and she strained to filter out other conversations and the ramblings of the rodeo announcer. "That's nice, honey, but I'm trying to watch," said a woman's voice.

"But, Mommy," the little girl pleaded, "its right over there, on top of the cover."

Nelson raised on tiptoes while grabbing a pole for support. As she did so, she peered out between various pairs of shoes to see across the arena. The mother of the child apparently did not look, because if she did, she would have seen the dark shadow of a hundred-pound bat slinking back from the edge of the awning covering the stands. "Holy Mother Mary, another one!" she whispered aloud in horror.

Nelson turned to run to tell the others when she heard something snort from directly behind her.

Two big brown eyes were staring fixedly at her. Her heart pounded wildly and she stepped back only to bang her head on one of the lower set of bleachers. She winced but noticed that now several pairs of eyes were locked in on her. She recognized them to belong to the young steers that were being roped earlier in the rodeo. They were much bigger up close, probably a couple hundred pounds with heads coming to her chest. They had been stored under the bleachers during the rodeo.

"Go away," she said softly, as if waving off an annoying butterfly. She didn't want to sound threatening; she knew nothing of cattle. The steers merely stood there, blinking dumbly.

She took a step toward the opening from which she had entered. They began to follow. "Stay there, nice . . . cows," she said, putting her hand out like a crossing guard during traffic hour.

"You all right?" said a low voice from behind her.

Without turning, she said, "I just don't want them to follow me, that's all."

"Okay," said the man standing behind her. Without warning, Nelson saw an empty beer can flying over her head. "Git!" screamed the man with a slight drawl. Instantly, the steers jumped back and moved to the farthest part of the enclosure, huddling with each other again under the shadows of the bleachers. She turned to the stranger to give her thanks.

Fitzpatrick was smiling at her impishly as he stood with his thumbs clinging to a huge belt buckle on his waist; he even had a piece of grass in his teeth. Nelson fumed with anger and blushed with embarrassment. She couldn't say anything except, "I just saw another one!"

∞

They looked everywhere but couldn't find a trace of the animal on the rodeo grounds. The announcer had just thanked everyone for coming out, and people were filing out to the parking lot. It was impossible to navigate through the throng; the FBI agents attempted to get to higher ground by getting back up to the top bleachers. They found nothing; it was gone.

"They're coming into town," Johnson said seriously, "and looks like it's not just to snatch a person."

"Yeah," Fitzparick snorted, "they're coming for dinner and a show!"

They had all been thinking it. Animals didn't perch to watch a rowdy mass of people and music unless they weren't afraid. "Let's notify the authorities," Nelson said, shaking her head. "Maybe the night patrol will see something."

∞

Sherman Hinkley was definitely not human anymore. Flight had come easily enough; he had run into two traffic lights swinging from wires before realizing that he really didn't have to follow the paths of roads. Luckily, no one saw him. He swooped over houses and buildings then dove low through alley ways and even attempted a dive roll. He felt like he was on a roller coaster but on his own power and he could choose to go anywhere. Instead of teenagers screaming loudly or the clanking of metal cars on rails, he only had the rush of wind echoing in his ears. He could focus his attention and listen in on other's thoughts. It was amazing and scary. He had to also try to block out the white noise of so many thoughts coming into his head at one time. But he realized that even this seemed to be easy for him after only a little while.

It was risky, but Sherman was practicing his flying abilities and just mastering some loops when he began getting the thought patterns of people in the rodeo. It intrigued him, and he decided to perch himself on the tin awning of the stadium. He thought that with all the action happening down below, no one would be looking up to see a looming shadow peering over the edge. He had been closing his light-sensitive eyes and concentrating on thought patterns when he detected the little girl spotting him across the arena.

He could hear her thoughts even within the crowd. He was thankful Mom wasn't paying attention. He pushed back from the edge, turned, and launched himself into the night sky. *That was too close. I must find Daniel,* he thought. *Tonight.*

Chapter 19

History of a Queen

Sherman flew through the night, following the highway that led to Daniel and Erin Simm's house. They lived far from town, and he felt more at ease as there were few lights. It was late, and he only flew over a couple of cars driving down the road far below, their headlights floating like a pair of glowing eyes surrounded by thick darkness. Glowing eyes like his. It had only been hours since the transformation, his mind was drained from so many thought patterns that had been flooding his head and his body began to ache from the fatigue of flying. The initial high of feeling like a superhero was quickly wearing off. He had to see a friend, desperation was creeping into his thoughts of his future and what life would now be like, coupled with a cold fear of how he was going to survive.

The Jackson Hole Airport and its plethora of lights shone below, he peered around for any airplanes, realizing that he could actually run into a flying plane up here. The night sky was dark and empty of any lights. He had always loved flying in airplanes, and had fantasies of flying without aid like most people, but now it was true. The feeling of isolation as he flew in the dark sky felt imposing and ominous, a far cry from sitting on an airplane watching a movie and eating overpriced sandwiches. The stars twinkled as if flirting with him to come and fly among them. He toyed with the idea of how high could he get before the air would be too scant of oxygen for him to breath, then his thoughts turned to destinations he'd always wanted to go but never could find the time or afford it. Now, flying was free, he could go anywhere! The sense of freedom was immense and seemed limitless. *I could fly to the Amazon or the Yukon tonight if I wanted,* he thought. His rambling dreams eased the sick feelings of his prospects at being a giant mind-reading bat for the rest of his life.

The Simm's house was coming into view and he could see lights were still on. *This is going to be tough to explain*, he thought. *Better start from a distance.*

He decided it would be best to perch himself somewhere outside of the house and try to contact Daniel via his mind and attempt to set the idea of his circumstances firmly into Daniel's cranium before he actually faced him to avoid too much shock. He was just preparing to land when he saw the truck in the driveway and someone was standing there.

"No, wait," Erin was saying. "Darwin, come back!"

Sherman saw Erin with Daniel quickly joining her looking up into the sky, screaming. Instantly, he saw the black shape of a huge bat swing around as he approached the house. The familiar glowing eyes focused on him; it screamed a bloodcurdling shriek and charged him. Sherman swerved and dived low, narrowly missing the attack, rows of white fangs snapping at him as it passed.

He was new at flight and had just gotten the hang of doing a few basic maneuvers; airborne dogfights were way out of his league. He was scared for his life; this creature wanted to kill him, he could sense it.

"Stop!" Erin yelled from below.

Darwin pulled up, breaking off his attack dive and wheeled around. This time, he was hovering in midair, fluttering his wings and staring fixedly at Sherman who was trying to regain some flight control and land without hurting himself.

With a loud metallic thud, Sherman landed square on the top of the cab of Erin's truck. Both Erin and Daniel leapt back; Daniel had a flashlight that he raised and placed the beam of light on Sherman's head. "There's another one, Erin!" he yelled. Daniel looked frantically from side to side then grabbed a large fallen tree branch and held it aloft as if he were ready to receive a baseball pitch.

"Wait!" Erin said, holding a hand to Daniel. "Let's just wait, okay?"

Daniel was breathing heavily; he reluctantly lowered the stick but still remained rigid and poised for anything. Erin directed her mind like she did with Darwin. *Are you friendly?*

You have no idea, Erin. It's me . . . Sherman!

Erin let out a breath and wobbled; she grabbed Daniel's arm to steady herself. Daniel held her. Quickly, Sherman sent thought messages that described his transformation and his abilities. Erin's mind seemed so receptive to his thoughts; Sherman decided it was better if Erin translated for him as she explained, in words, to Daniel.

Upon the final sentence, Daniel lurched for the truck and leaned heavily upon it. Sherman sat still on the cab staring down at his friend with glowing eyes. Suddenly, a wave of sadness swept over him. The idea of not being able to hang out with his long-time friend as they had done for years occurred to him. No more family events, experimental cooking for the kids, pubs and watching the games. His life as Sherman Hinkley ended tonight. Sherman realized–sensed–that Daniel was thinking the same thing.

Meanwhile, Darwin, though free, remained two hundred feet in the night sky. His dark shape could be just seen fluttering among the twinkling stars.

Far below, in a pine tree not far from the driveway, sat Dot and Ralph. "Why did we just set that monster free?" Dot asked, feeling sick to his stomach.

"It asked us to," Ralph said simply. "At least it didn't eat us, right?"

Dot didn't know what to think. Since the narrow escape from the cliff, they had been trying to stay away from anything looking like a bat, even the small ones. "Ralph, maybe we should migrate," he squeaked.

Dot looked up and saw Darwin, hovering over the driveway, suddenly fold his wings and dive toward the other creature sitting on top of the truck. Another loud metallic thud followed by a scream of terror echoed in the night.

Darwin stood mantling over Sherman who was cowering with his wings held over his head like two huge umbrellas. *Darwin! This is a friend of mine. You must not harm him, please!* Erin transmitted the thought urgently.

Darwin took a small step back. The truck creaked. He folded his wings slowly while giving a piercing glare toward Sherman. Erin sent the story of her friend through thoughts and images, trying to explain how this creature was not one of them but was a human only hours ago.

Darwin's face looked forlorn. *It is happening again,* he thought back to Erin and this time transmitted his words to both Sherman and Daniel. *Only this time, she has awoken too early.*

Erin stepped closer and verbally voiced her question with a look of horror on her face, "Darwin, what are you saying?"

Darwin bowed his head and his strikingly glowing blue eyes closed to slits. *She has not had her full sleep and is not at her full strength. That is why I have been able to stay free of her.*

"Why, Darwin," Erin urged, "why isn't she at her full strength?"

What is our time?

"You mean time of day? It's about ten thirty at night," Erin said.

No, what is the time? This time, the thought felt more strained.

"You mean what is the year?" Erin said with understanding. "We're in two thousand twelve."

A look of amazement fell onto Darwin's face. *She has only slept five hundred years!*

"What does that mean?" Daniel said impatiently. Erin touched his arm and stepped forward. "If she can change Sherman, that means she can change any of us?" Erin prompted.

Darwin nodded.

Sherman lowered his wings; he jolted them upright to look up at Darwin. *Were you human too?* he asked, focusing his thoughts.

Darwin nodded again. *My entire tribe was changed by her.*

Erin approached Darwin fearlessly and looked directly into his blank eyes. "Darwin," she commanded, "you must tell us everything."

∞

An hour had passed; Erin and Daniel had gotten fleece jackets. Darwin had told them that his queen was weakened each time she changed someone into an image of her. It was like giving a part of her; therefore, she needed to sleep once she was depleted. They learned that the queen needed thousands of years to rejuvenate her strength and that the last time she was active was in the fifteenth century.

"Where was she then?" Daniel asked.

She is not from this world but comes from the stars. She crash-landed and became stranded and alone. She told us that she was chased from the north and flew across large waters to arrive here, on this land.

"Is that when she changed you and your tribe?" Erin asked.

Darwin nodded. *She told us that there were many creatures in the north, birds that forced her to leave. She tried to change creatures into the likenesses of her to combat them, eventually finding people worked the best. However, her initial attempts ended badly. Those that did not die became grotesque and monstrous, only partially transforming and feeding on other people, drinking their blood.*

"Wait a minute," Erin interjected. "You're saying she started in the north, across the ocean, meaning somewhere in Europe or possibly Russia. She tried to change others to her race but it didn't work out, however, those that lived continued to spread?"

"Erin," Daniel said, "are you thinking of old legends, of . . . vampires?"

"It fits," Erin exclaimed. "Where do all these stories come from? Somewhere, someone must have had an experience for it to be such a pervasive legend. What if she started it all, five hundred years ago, Europe, that's where legend says vampires originated, right? Transylvania!"

"Why not werewolves too while you're at it!" Daniel said, throwing his hands in the air.

"Sure," Erin said sincerely. "Look at Darwin's face. You're telling me you don't see some resemblance?"

Daniel said nothing. It did fit, to a point, but it was all so much to take in that his brain needed time to process it all. "So now she's come to North America, then what?"

She found the same trouble, just different species. Raptors of all kinds mounted a resistance, and she was almost killed. That's when she found my village and decided to try again, only she must have learned from her mistakes, because this time the transformation was complete, so much so that she could also control us with her mind, making us a willing and serving army. The effort left her weak. She sought a place where she thought no one or nothing could find us and bore an entrance under the ice. She plugged the hole in hopes that she would get her needed time to rest.

"But that didn't happen," Daniel said. "The ice melted much sooner than she anticipated."

"Global climate change," Erin whispered. "The ice melted faster than she anticipated. Sherman was right!"

At this Sherman nodded vigorously; he even managed a smile, showing off his rows of glimmering white teeth.

"Darwin," Erin said thoughtfully, "is she aware that she has come out of her hibernation too soon?"

I'm sure she senses that she is not at full strength, but I think she does not know yet what the present time is. She has been recruiting again thinking that she will have strength enough to finish her army and destroy those that forced her underground.

"So how do we kill it?" Daniel said with a yawn.

I have met two creatures that have told me of a bird with unnatural speed. I think this is the same bird that injured me.

"And how can this bird do anything?" Daniel pressed.

The queen's original form is not like me. All I can tell you is that its weakest state is when it is divided. It holds the shape of a flying queen only for a few hours when it needs. If something were to split it on impact, maybe several times . . .

"You think this will kill it?" Erin asked.

Darwin nodded and reached out to Dot and Ralph, calling them to come to him. A branch of a tree wavered slightly, and soon, a small owl and a vulture landed nervously on the hood of the truck. Erin and Daniel stood dumbfounded. "This has got to be the craziest night I've ever had," Daniel said staring at the two birds.

We are going to search for this bird known as Blurr, Darwin thought to the group.

Suddenly, Sherman, who had been listening intently, burst in, *Wait! Is there any possibility of changing back if this queen dies?*

Everyone heard the question in their mind and waited for Darwin to answer. The large bat stood, wings wrapped around his body, eyes showing that he was seriously contemplating the answer. *I do not know, but I hope there is a chance something will happen.*

Chapter 20

The Council of Birds

Well, this is it, Blurr thought as she followed Ki'ta on their final approach into the lair of the hawk's clan.

"Look," voiced the giant hawk with admiration. "That is my home."

The early evening cast the last rays of sunlight over a small valley nestled within two towering hills. Cottonwood trees mixed with pine trees covered the area as a flowing brook meandered its way down the middle. To Blurr, this was as peaceful and tranquil a place as she had ever seen. Drawing closer to the trees, she noticed several nests, many of them empty.

Blurr and Ki'ta leveled just at the height of the trees when suddenly numerous shrieks were heard from both sides. Blurr's heart pounded as she readied for an attack. "Don't worry," Ki'ta said, seeing Blurr's angst. "Those are only the nest guards."

Just then, four hawks swooped into view and flanked them, two on each side. Ki'ta acknowledged them with a nod of the head while Blurr looked nervously from side to side. The nest guards were resolute in face and demeanor; they shadowed every move the two birds made, and it wasn't until Ki'ta led Blurr to a nest that they broke off their escort.

"This is my nest," Ki'ta said, landing on the edge of a large circular flat of twigs interwoven to present a stable platform. It was clean and looked inviting to Blurr; she had never been in a nest to her recollection. The fragrance of wood sitting in the sun was strong; she would remember this smell, this feeling of a bird's home.

"Normally," Ki'ta said, looking out at the expanse of trees, "we nest further from each other to give our race some room to live and hunt. But since the demons, we've moved to our traditional safe ground in hopes that our numbers will fend off our enemy. It hasn't worked very well."

Blurr listened from behind with extreme interest when she saw a formation of large birds approaching. There must of have been at least twenty, flying in a tight group. Blurr saw the nest guards zoom out to join them, flanking each side of the group as they did with her and Ki'ta. It wasn't long before Blurr realized it was a band of eagles, and she gulped inadvertently.

"More and more come every day," Ki'ta said looking up at the eagles. "Owls too."

"You have owls here too?" Blurr asked hopefully.

"All kinds," Ki'ta said, still tracking the eagles as they whooshed overhead and landed among the trees. "Everyone has been suffering these days. They know that the only way to survive is to join forces, even if we have been . . . enemies in the past."

Blurr had a fleeting thought of Dot and Ralph showing up here, finding safety among the brethren of other raptors. She dismissed the idea quickly, knowing enough about Dot that he would only be around so many large, potentially hungry raptors if he had no other option. *That is*, she thought, *if he were still alive.*

"Tonight, you will speak to the council of elders," Ki'ta said. "Tell them what you saw, what they are like to fight. Maybe we will be able to mount an attack that will be more effective than in the past."

At the thought of standing in front of a council of raptors, Blurr felt an eruption of nervousness. She did not want to look like a fool and was afraid that the other raptors would think she was. She was young, with little experience in the wild, and here she was to present her accidental collision with the giant bat as something important for them to use. She thought about leaving. *I could fly out of here right now and never look back*, she thought. But something inside of her held her fast. Was it a sense of loyalty to Ki'ta?

I've only just met her, Blurr thought. *How can I really trust her? She's a hawk!*

Blurr's internal dialogue was severed when Ki'ta voiced, "I must go and tell the council you are here. I will come get you when they are ready." Ki'ta took a small hop to the edge of the nest and was ready to leap when she stopped in mid-motion and whispered over her shoulder, "Thank you, falcon, for this. Tomorrow we will look for your friends."

Ki'ta leapt off the nest's edge and flew out of sight among the canopy of trees in the distance.

∞

What was a virtually cloudless day had changed as night approached. Far in the distance, large gray clouds were forming, promising the chance of a wet evening. Blurr hated to get her feathers wet.

Blurr went over her experience in her mind, trying to think of ways that she thought the council would benefit and she would not look like an idiot. She watched the gathering storm clouds; they were descending quickly as the last rays of light faded to shades of gray. She saw movement among the trees and noticed Ki'ta flying quickly toward her. *Too late to back out now,* she thought. Her only hope of rescue from this presentation now was that if the storm forced the council to delay.

"It is time," Ki'ta said, swooping low over Blurr's head and leading the way. Blurr leapt off the nest and followed; now that it was darker, she noticed the tree branches were painfully hard to avoid. The two birds zigzagged among the trees until they came to a circular clearing where large trees loomed with their thick branches bowing toward the center.

Instantly, Blurr's anxiety returned to full strength; she saw hundreds of raptors of all kinds within the surrounding canopy. She could feel all eyes on her as Ki'ta led her through the center of the clearing and to a large branch on the opposite side. They landed together, and Ki'ta turned to face the others. Though the sun had gone behind the mountains, there was a lasting gloom as if the land was grasping at the remaining light, forcing it to stay and linger for just a little longer.

Blurr could only make out shapes of bodies in the trees on the other side; those that were on her flank, she could still see easily. A large owl sat only feet away; its giant yellow eyes peering at her suspiciously. On her other side was an impressive looking eagle, the contrast of the white head and tail with the dark body looked even more so in the ebbing light. There were others: small owls that reminded Blurr of Dot, many types of hawks of all colors, and more eagles. The one thing that was plain, at least from her viewpoint, was the absence of any falcons. *Why was any of her kind not represented here?* she thought.

Her mind began to ponder the various reasons: *too few in number, too far away to know about this gathering, too hated by others, or what is it–that they were too scared to fight?*

She didn't have a chance to think any longer as Ki'ta broke the nervous silence. "My cousins," she began, "I've asked you here on a most pressing issue. There is a new hunter among us. Many of you have felt the might of these demons and have lost your chicks or even your mates. Food is dwindling. Where there was a balance for us all to be here to hunt and live, now there is nothing left. We have had our differences in the past, sometimes we've been mortal enemies. We cannot afford to be separated into different clans now. We must unite as one and overthrow this enemy that threatens our very existence. We must come together. We must fight!"

Ki'ta ended and fell silent; many mumblings from the crowd ensued interspersed with short cries of discontent. Then a large owl stepped out further on her branch. "If I may," she announced in an almost dreamlike voice. "As leader of the great grey owl clan, I feel compelled to say that I agree with Ki'ta, there is a scourge upon our land, and if we don't act quickly, we will lose it . . . perhaps forever."

"You've always been on Ki'ta's side, Threy," screamed a great horned owl from Blurr's left, "but there are others of us that do not share your affection for these day hunters."

The owl was rough-looking, like she had been in many battles and lived to tell about it. Her voice was also rough and gravely, like sifting rock through a screen. It was here that Blurr realized that everyone at the council was female. *Could all clans be guided by females? What did that make her?* She would have to tuck that question away and ask Ki'ta when there was the chance.

"I know, Boldree, but this is a time where if we don't unite as one, we all lose together," replied Threy in a hypnotically calm voice. Instantly, Boldree settled and did not say more.

"Hunters!" cried Ki'ta. "Threy is right, if we don't work together, we will all lose together. I have brought you someone who has fought these creatures and has survived. I want you to listen to what she has to say." There was some more discordant muffling, but no one protested.

Ki'ta looked at Blurr, as did Threy. Blurr felt paralyzed. Her falcon legs would not move; it was as if her talons were planted firmly within the branch she was perching upon and decided that that was where they were going to stay until the tree fell down. Blurr saw Ki'ta slightly flick her head as if to cue her to enter the stage. Blurr's nerves were all firing at once; she knew the hawk needed someone to come through for her. Blurr would never be able to consider herself honorable if she fled now; she had to face the council and hopefully tell them something useful.

"I have seen and fought with these creatures," Blurr said, trying to stifle her nervousness. "They are as big as an eagle and have the night vision of an owl." To this, there were many whispers among the crowd; Blurr could feel all attention was on her now. "I have seen where they hide and have watched how they fly."

"What are we going to do?" exclaimed the eagle at Blurr's side. "My eagles can go one on one with demons during the day, but we are swamped by their numbers, and we are no match for them at night."

"How are we to fight such a hunter?" asked another.

"Falcon, how many did you see?" asked an older hawk sitting quietly within the crowd.

Blurr looked at her concerned face and reluctantly said, "Thousands." To this, there was an uproar of conversation among the different clans. It took some time for Ki'ta and Threy to calm the crowd down.

"I have one more thing to say," Blurr said, a thought occurred to her and her confidence rose slightly. "They have a soft underbelly, lined with fur but easily penetrated by talons."

"You know this to be true?" Boldree hissed.

"Yes," Blurr said. "I . . . collided with one and sunk my talons deep within its underside. The wounds seemed to weaken it enough . . ." Blurr's voice trailed, she was going to say "to be bound," but that would require her to explain her interaction with the ravens, which she thought would surely make her look the fool. Instead, she said, "to lie disabled until I left it the next morning."

The crowd exploded with hoots and cries and demands for action. Blurr looked over to Ki'ta; she was staring intently at her. This knowledge would be crucial if they were to mount a defense. The hawk nodded respectfully toward Blurr and turned to address the crowd. She listened as Ki'ta spoke to the elders of each clan; the council meeting lasted for hours. There was talk of strategy and timing, of when to attack and where, then finally of sending scouts to find the exact location of the nest, assuming they had one.

Blurr had done her job; she gave them something useful and managed to not look like a young naïve bird. A glimmer of confidence glowed within her; she felt good about her presentation and felt that Ki'ta thought it was good as well. The council was ending; Blurr was sleepy and just wanted to drift into dreams of a problem-free world for just a little while. Ki'ta nudged her. "It's over, Blurr," she said, looking very content. "Thanks to you, we have made plans, and you have given us hope that we can stand a chance against them."

An older owl, one that Blurr had seen at the council, guided them safely back to their nest. It was very dark and owls were leading the day hunters back to nests for the night. They settled together in the large bed of twigs, resting comfortably. Blurr thought about where she had started her day and how it had ended. Life in the wild was very unpredictable; she was growing to like it, and it didn't even rain.

Chapter 21

A Turn of Events

It had been three days since the council; Blurr had gotten to know the surrounding area well on her daily sojourns. Ki'ta was mostly busy with the council, deciding how and who would be going to the demon's nest to assess a better attack. It was hot, but some plumes of clouds promised late afternoon cover from the penetrating sun. Food was scarce; she didn't see much around and had to fly far just to find decent flocks of anything she could hunt. The mumblings around Ki'ta's home nest was that everyone was forced to fly far and pickings were slim even at far distances.

She had lots of time to think about Dot and Ralph; she had gone out several times with hawks that Ki'ta said were trustworthy but had not found a trace of either one of them. Blurr's heart fell with each passing day; the realization that she would never see her friends again was something she convinced herself that she had to accept.

Blurr had aligned herself with the track of forest that was stopped abruptly by the canyon walls on each side. She had come to know this forest well as it was the entrance to Ki'ta's home nesting grounds. She had only gone a little way into the canyon when she noticed she was not joined by the usual escort. The canyon was strangely quiet this afternoon.

It was at that moment that her keen falcon eyes caught movement below in the canopy of cottonwoods. The motion was quick and jerky as if something was trying hard not to be seen. She circled back around for another pass, this time flying lower so that her belly was just barely missing the topmost branches. *There you are. So what are you? Prey or predator?* she thought to herself.

She had become so focused on tracing the movement of her mysterious quarry that she spooked when suddenly her body was covered in shadow.

She weaved to the left. She wanted so desperately to barrel roll, to face her surprise attacker and give it a full display of her talons, but she was so close to the treetops that she couldn't afford the moment's loss of altitude and crash into the upper branches of the forest. The shadow hung on her with every bob and weave; Blurr dove into the labyrinth of foliage.

Branches and leaves seemed to want to trip her up; she flapped hard while using her tail as a rudder just narrowly avoiding serious injury on several sharp-looking branches. She stole a moment to look back. *Surely I've lost him by now!*

Blurr's heart sank when, glancing back, she saw the huge looming figure of a black demon swooping in and out of the trees; in the confining forest, the creature's wings slashed through smaller branches, exploding leaves in all directions. Its glowing blue eyes were narrowed and focused on her. The wrinkled snout, accented with rows of teeth, was prominent, though to Blurr the face did not appear aggressive, but rather one of exertion as it worked hard to not lose her.

When she turned to get her bearing ahead, she reeled in horror as another demon was sitting on a branch directly in front of her. "Two!" She breathed, her body aching from the taxing beating of her wings. Feeling trapped, she resolved that she would have to fight. *At least I may be able to take one of them with me*, she confirmed as she pushed herself to gain speed.

She could not go as fast as she could in a dive and she thought at this speed there was no way she could knock the creature off the branch. But that wasn't her intention. She saw the perching demon come to the realization that she was going on the offensive and his glowing blue eyes widened in surprise. Blurr saw it look side to side nervously but it did not light from the branch.

She would sink her talons into it's soft hairy belly and do as much damage as possible before she would be ripped to shreds by the other. Her target was panicking; it fluttered its wings indecisively as if it couldn't decide whether to fly or not. As Blurr made her final push, the demon cowered and holding its wings up as a shield, it turned its head, bracing for the impact.

"Blurr, wait!" came a tiny squeaking voice from nearby. "It's us, don't attack."

Blurr wobbled, her concentration blown. *That sounded like Dot!*

Just then, another rather large dark figure hopped into view on the branch right next to the cowering demon; it was Ralph.

Blurr shrieked with surprise; it couldn't be true—Ralph alive and on the same side as a demon? Nevertheless, at the last second, Blurr swerved to barely miss the mesh of dark wings held aloft; she could see it was trembling in fear. *This creature is not like the others*, Blurr thought as she passed over it.

Meanwhile, the dark shadow that was pursuing her landed next to Ralph and the terrified demon, whom she could see now was much smaller and looked more frail than the other. Blurr circled around, avoiding two trees, and landed on a branch far enough away to make a hasty retreat if necessary.

"Hi, Blurr," Ralph echoed cordially through the trees as if they had only just seen each other recently.

"Ralph?" Blurr called. "Is that really you?" She saw the bird nod happily, still standing comfortably next to the huge dark shadows of wings and teeth.

"Are you all right?" Blurr asked tentatively. Again, Ralph nodded. "Where is Dot?"

"I'm here!" Dot said coming into view, his camouflage blending in perfectly with the surrounding forest. He had to move in order for her to see him.

"Dot," Blurr said suspiciously, pointing her beak at the demons, "if you're both okay, why are they with you?"

"It's a bit of a long story, Blurr," Dot said, looking up at the larger of the two demons. "You're going to have to trust me on this one."

Blurr sat motionless, trying to process the fact that her friends were alive, but her sense of elation was squashed by the apparent alliance to these terrible creatures, to the enemy of every raptor in the land! She spent the next few moments in silence, internally debating as to whether this was really happening, and if it was, could she trust her long-lost friends?

The others seemed to have sensed her deliberation and remained quiet, patiently waiting and trying not to look at her. To Blurr, they looked pathetically transparent as they were all trying to look casual as if they were just admiring the scenery. However, she could feel a sense of urgency in all of them, like they desperately wanted to get going but were trying hard not to look it.

Finally, Blurr spoke, "Okay, Dot," she said, "I will listen to what you have to say, but only you and Ralph may come with me. *They* must stay here."

At this, the smaller demon looked nervous at the conditions set by Blurr while the other stayed motionless, like a huge dark statue, blinking its blank blue eyes occasionally. "We'll follow you," Dot squeaked, and both he and Ralph leapt off the branches they had been perched upon and followed Blurr to another huge cottonwood on the edge of the forest. Blurr figured there was a nice bit of open space for them to escape, just in case this turned ill.

"I can't believe you're alive!" exclaimed Blurr.

"Neither can I," Dot said, nodding. "We watched you as all those Pshotee went chasing you."

"Those what?" Blurr interrupted.

Dot smiled. "Pshotee," he said, "that's what they call themselves."

"And how do you know this?" Blurr asked, her suspicions rising.

"That," Dot said with a sigh, "is even a longer story. But for now, I'll give you the short version." Dot told Blurr about their escape that night, their aimless wandering just trying to keep out of sight, then their chance meeting with Darwin and Sherman.

"The frightened one is called Sherman?" Blurr clarified.

"It's a human name I guess, that's what he was until he was bitten by the queen of the Pshotee, then he changed into one of them. Darwin too, but he was changed a long time ago. Anyway, he says he doesn't want to go by Sherman anymore since he's not human. He wants to be called Batman, stupid, huh?"

Blurr was trying to take it all in, but it was difficult. If something gets bitten, it changes into one of them, a Pshotee? She shook her head. "How do you know all this?" she asked.

"Right," Dot said, choosing his words carefully. "They think their words into our heads—images really—we can either say or think back to them. They understand everything right away!"

"Even the one who was just changed?" Blurr said, looking around as if someone might be listening to their conversation.

"Yes, well," Dot said, "once he stopped crying after he learned that he was a Pshotee forever, he got better at thinking to us. Humans are strange, aren't they?"

Blurr knew a lot about humans and she would agree that they are strange, but this idea of humans changing to Pshotee was something she could not come to believe. "If these Pshotee are friends of yours," Blurr said accusingly, "then why did the larger one attack me?"

"He was trying to communicate to you by mind," Dot said quickly, sensing some hostility from the falcon. "He told me that he could not reach into your mind. He couldn't tell you his intentions, so he tried to direct you to us. We have been searching for you for days!"

"Searching for me?" Blurr said, still trying to put all the pieces together so they made sense to her; however, she was going to need more explanation. She let Dot talk more about what he'd learned about the Pshotee, about how they could read thoughts, think images into others minds, even control creatures' actions. "But only when they have to," he had included quickly. He also told her how the Pshotee queen had recruited others by inflicting wounds that would change creatures into those of her race; most were humans because the queen preferred them.

"Darwin thinks that you would have the speed to kill the queen," Dot said happily. "He also seemed happy that your mind is blocked from his abilities . . . something about that being an advantage when facing the queen!"

Just then, Blurr heard the war cries of many hawks not far from where they left Darwin and Batman. Urgently, she said, "We've got to go your friends, the hawks will kill them if they can!"

∞

Moments later, Blurr saw that the nest guard had returned to their posts and the hawks had flushed the two Pshotee out of the trees and were trying to gut the bellies of each by flying hard and fast with talons outstretched. Two of them were swarming around Darwin, but his flight maneuvers were making it difficult for the hawks to get a clear shot at the belly. Batman, however, was floundering. Blurr saw at least three narrow escapes by the lesser Pshotee; dumb luck seemed to be on his side.

"Stop!" Blurr cried, flying among the fray. The hawks ignored her cry, dodging around her.

"Move aside, falcon," shrieked one of the hawks. "We must protect our nest!"

"They are here," screamed Blurr, "to offer aid!"

Both hawks looked confused at first but decided to continue their relentless flybys trying frantically to kill the smaller one. Blurr realized they had stopped listening to her. She whipped around and dove, instantly catching one hawk off guard and sending him spiraling down to the trees. The other hawk attacked her, but she easily swerved, rolled, and clenched his foot in her talons. With as much care as she could, she whipped the other hawk downward, releasing her grip. She hoped her talons didn't sink too far into the hawk's foot.

She was taking a big chance siding with the demons. After this display, the hawks would be her enemy forever, and she would never see Ki'ta again if they could not convince her of their intentions.

Blurr turned toward the other two hawk guards only to find them flying in unison off toward the home nest. Darwin flew down to join Blurr; Dot also joined them. Darwin's ears twitched as he looked to Dot. "He's sent them home," Dot said, translating Darwin's thoughts, "to try and convince others that we're coming and what our intentions are."

"How can he make them do that?" Blurr asked as she stared at the ominous figure, a sense of amazement coupled with welling dread coated her mind. *Controlling other's minds will be one huge disadvantage for the hawks,* she thought.

"I can't really explain how," Dot said, slightly shrugging in midflight. "They have this way with minds . . . except yours apparently."

Ralph caught up to them. *A vulture, an owl, a falcon, and two demons*, she thought, shaking her head and looking at her companions. *We'll be lucky if we're not killed right away!*

They flew only a short way when they were joined by legions of hawks, large owls, and eagles to escort them into the home nest. As they flew surrounded by an army of raptors who all seemed ready to finish them off right here, Blurr knew that they were going to have only one chance to persuade Ki'ta that these two emissaries of the Pshotee were needed to defeat the queen and her horde.

"You are to follow me," shrieked a dark hawk, swooping in front of Blurr, taking suspicious glances at Darwin and Batman.

The guide led his entourage over several stands of forest. Blurr knew enough about the area to know that they were not heading toward the council tree; this was new. They flew over many nests, all empty, and into an offshoot of the canyon. It was narrow, forcing everyone to fly in single file. Blurr was just behind their escort, she glanced behind her to see Darwin trying to avoid scraping his wings against the rocky sides with every wingbeat. Another quick glance behind her confirmed that the raptor army was following closely behind them.

The walls continued to narrow until there was barely any room to fly. Just then, the hawk guide extended his wings and rolled a quarter turn so that his wing tips aligned vertically as he soared through a thin gap of space left between the walls of rock. Blurr and the others followed suit. They soared through the gap and burst into an impressive opening of the canyon. Smooth stone slabs barren of plant life loomed on all sides, making a large amphitheater and arching above to where the rock almost touched, forming an enclosure. *Only one way out of here*, Blurr observed. *They're not taking any chances.*

Blurr's eyes widened. She saw that hundreds of raptors were already here and more were spilling through the gap behind them. Their guide had disappeared into the crowd, but he was not needed any longer. Blurr knew where to go as she saw a large flat stone resting just below a ledge on the rock wall. Ki'ta was perched on the ledge along with others, waiting.

Blurr, Dot, Ralph, Darwin, and Batman landed on the slab of flat sandstone looking up at Ki'ta and the large owl named Threy as well as the eagle Blurr recognized from the council. Like judges looking down at the accused, they all had faces of stern disbelief; Blurr noticed that Ki'ta bore the face not only of harsh criticism but shock at Blurr's betrayal. Blurr felt sick to her stomach; it was the worst she had ever felt in her life.

"You have come here, demons," Ki'ta said, "saying that you are here to help us."

"Let me expl–" Blurr started.

"Silence!" Ki'ta screamed then hissed, "I want to hear from *them.*"

"Excuse me," Dot said with as much reverence as he could muster. "Please forgive me, but they do not speak like we do. Would it be okay if I interpreted for them?" Blurr saw Dot bow low, his head almost touching the rock.

"You may, little one," Ki'ta said, nodding. She wore a fierce look upon her brow as if she were ready to leap down on them all.

"His name is Darwin," Dot began. "He is of the Pshotee and is here as an ally not against his own kind but against his queen."

"What's the difference?" asked the eagle in a low voice.

"He says," Dot responded as Darwin drew his gaze toward the eagle, "that his kind is made to be servants to the queen, that they only do her bidding. If given the choice, however, they would not harm your race . . . like him."

To this, there was an uproar among the gathering crowd of hundreds of birds perched anywhere there was space within the amphitheater. Ki'ta called for silence; it took several moments for them to become quiet.

"How do we know he is telling us the truth?" Threy asked solemnly.

Darwin turned his gaze to the owl, then Dot spoke, "I will give you my companion as collateral if I don't live up to my promise of aid to your race."

At this, many birds called out while Batman looked at Darwin with shock and a look of horror as he fidgeted on the stone perch.

"And you," Ki'ta said, her stern gaze now falling upon Blurr, "what do you offer as proof that you are still my friend and not a traitor?"

Every fiber of Blurr's being stung with Ki'ta's loss of faith in her. Her mind was soaked in desperation to say something that would be right and would make Ki'ta realize that Blurr was loyal to Ki'ta and her clan. Suddenly, she screamed for all to hear, "I will offer my life. I will go to the Pshotee and call them out to battle and then kill the queen . . . if I can!"

"You would do this alone, falcon?" Ki'ta asked, her voice softening.

"Yes," Blurr said firmly.

"Not alone," Ralph spoke, but this time with confidence and even grace; everyone looked at him in surprise. "I will go with her!"

"I'm going too!" squeaked Dot, jumping to Ralph's side.

Blurr stood. If everyone wasn't watching, she would have turned and hugged her companions. Just then, Dot stepped forward and said, "Darwin requests that he go as their guide. He says that he can get them into the cave and to the queen. He said it's vital that the queen come out to the battle. Once the queen is destroyed, the others will be lost without her control, and Darwin will be able to communicate to them that you are not enemies of Pshotee."

The mass of raptors screeched and whistled while Ki'ta, Threy, and the eagle conferred high on their altar of rock. Blurr could feel everyone, not just those on trial, but all the birds observing, fixedly staring at the three in anticipation of what the clan leaders were going to decide.

Finally, Ki'ta prepared to speak; she waited for the crowd's noise to die down. "We've decided. Based on the offerings of . . . our allies," she said, looking down upon Blurr, Dot, Ralph, Darwin and even Batman, "that they are to go to the demons . . . the Pshotee, and draw out the queen as we will assemble our armies of hawks, eagles, and owls. We will face our enemy in the sky!"

The crowd exploded with war cries of every nature. Ki'ta stood majestic and beautiful. Blurr swore she would never forget this image of her mentor and friend. She couldn't believe the turn of events. She thought that they were never going to survive this trial and now they were accepted as allies. The plan to go to the nest of Pshotee and somehow get the queen and all her horde to come out of their nest was however something she had not thought through.

Ki'ta turned her gaze back down to Blurr. She gave a small smile, and Blurr's heart leapt with joy. She knew she was prepared to do anything for Ki'ta and for Dot and Ralph. She meant it when she offered her life to her friends.

Chapter 22

Unforeseen Reinforcements

Ralph threw up two more times after they had discussed the plan of getting past the guards, confronting the queen and escaping the nest long enough to provide Blurr with the opportunity she needed to kill the queen. After the acceptance of the two Pshotee into the hawk clan's home nest, it seemed to Blurr that everyone was busy preparing for the coming battle. She noticed that it wasn't fear she felt passing over groups of raptors huddled together talking and discussing flight strategy, but excitement.

"It's because they feel like they have a chance to reclaim the sky again," Ki'ta had said the next morning. "They trust you and therefore trust your friends . . . even the two Pshotee."

Ki'ta had forgiven Blurr, and they had spent most of the night talking strategy with Darwin, Dot being the consummate translator. Darwin tried at first to send his thoughts into Ki'ta's mind directly, but every time he did, she felt dizzy and, as a courtesy, he stopped. Even though it took longer to communicate, Dot seemed to be very quick, even trying to add Darwin's interpreted feelings to his thoughts. "He cannot thank you enough for your clan's hospitality," Dot said with much affection. "He will honor your efforts with his life if need be."

The plan was simple, direct, and with little chance of survival as Blurr went over it again, "So how do we get through the caves if there is no light?" she asked.

"Darwin will guide us by thought," Dot said, "imprinting the turns, obstacles, and directions in our heads."

"That's nice for you," Blurr said, "but I thought Darwin couldn't get into my head!"

Dot paused. "Good point." He looked at Darwin in silence, both locked in each other's gaze, focused. A moment later, Dot turned. "He says that he is going to challenge the queen and you are to stay out of the cave and wait for her."

Blurr admitted that she did like the thought of not going into the abyss of the Pshotee's nest, but she did not like the fact that her friends were going in without her. "Why doesn't just Darwin go in and we all wait. Why do you and Ralph need to go in anyway!"

"If the challenge fails," Ralph said simply, "we are the backup plan."

"Which is what?" Blurr urged.

"We are the bait," Dot squeaked.

∞

The morning went quickly as more preparation took place. Among the trees, hawks, eagles, and owls all began to assemble according to clans, preening feathers and cleaning beaks and talons on tree branches. It was time for Blurr and the rest of her group to go.

Ki'ta had been busy most of the day with other affairs, mostly trying to organize clan leaders and making last-minute changes to flight plans and sequence of attacks. Blurr knew it would be hard for Ki'ta to break away, and when they lit from their perch without fanfare, the thought of never coming back and seeing Ki'ta again gripped her. She felt sad, and her body seemed heavy as if all her feathers had become wet and her wings were sluggish. Blurr imagined a bit more of a send-off.

Suddenly, a familiar cry sounded behind her. The group turned and saw Ki'ta leading what looked to be dozens of every kind of raptor flying in beautiful formations around her. Blurr turned and saw that the others were gaping at the spectacle while her heart bounced back, her body feeling revitalized. Instantly, she felt like she could take on the queen.

The parade of birds showered over them, calling in unison as each battalion rolled this way and that, crossing flight lines or narrowly missing each other, then converged into one large flock that split ahead, forming a V and allowing Blurr and the rest to fly in the center.

When at last the farewell escort dropped back, returning to finish preparing for battle, Ki'ta caught up and flew next to Blurr. "You didn't think I would let my little sister leave without saying good-bye, did you?" she said.

Blurr couldn't speak; she had no words to describe her feelings of joy and pride and her love for Ki'ta. She had a sister now; that meant she was part of a family. Ki'ta let the silence pass only a moment then commanded,

"Blurr of the falcon clan, you represent your race well and it will be an honor to fly and fight with you."

Blurr's mind cleared slightly; she was the only falcon among them, though at the moment she felt more like a hawk. She smiled back to Ki'ta. "Ki'ta, *rital* of the hawk clan, it is my honor that you are my sister, and I will be pleased to fly and fight with you."

Ki'ta's amber eyes locked a moment on hers, then she let out a short shriek and broke right to make a long arch, returning to her home nest. Blurr did not look back.

To have the advantage of daylight, they would have to hurry. Blurr, Dot, Ralph, and Darwin flew out of the rolling hills of the hawk's home nesting grounds and back into the flat sagebrush lands that preceded the Teton Mountain Range. They were in full view of anyone that may be looking up, but they needed to make time and scurrying Darwin from tree stand to tree stand would take too long.

"There is the human path!" Dot called.

They all looked down, noticing that there were no cars visible on the lone highway stretching out below; all breathed a sigh. However, just then, a truck appeared from a small parking lot surrounded by trees, followed by a brown sedan. At first, the group paid it no attention, their minds thinking of the task at hand. It wasn't until Ralph made the comment, "I think those things are trying to follow us," that they all started to focus on the ground.

"They just turned again." Dot screamed, "You're right, Ralph, they are trying to follow us!"

Blurr turned, noticing for the first time a thin dark wire extending from Darwin's back. "What's that?" she said. Dot adjusted to get right above Darwin who tried to soar steadily. "I don't know, but there is a little flashing red light on it."

They continued to fly toward the cliffs just ahead, the shadows of the tall peaks passing over them. There was a sudden drop in temperature, and Blurr shivered at the abrupt change.

"I can't see them now," Blurr said, scanning below. The road could no longer go in their direction; if the humans were to continue to follow, they would have to be on foot.

"Oh no," Dot said quietly. "Darwin just got a faint thought pattern from Erin."

"What is an Erin?" Blurr asked.

"Erin is the human that Darwin can speak with the easiest. She healed his wounds."

"And?" Blurr prompted.

"Darwin says that Erin put something on his back that allows her to follow him," Dot finished.

"Are you saying that those humans are going to try to follow us to the Pshotee nest?" Blurr asked; her mind was whirling with having to deal with Pshotee and humans.

"There's more," Dot added tenderly. "They brought several humans with them."

Chapter 23

Challenge Delivered

Blurr could see the cliff face where her first encounter with the Pshotee took place; it was not a pleasant memory. Little did she know how that one night was going to change the course of her life.

"Darwin says the entrance is just beyond that field of rubble, at the ice's edge," Dot said, flying just under her. Ralph was soaring above all of them while Darwin coasted at Blurr's side. She felt so small compared to him, and even though she now felt she could trust him a little, his appearance and size were still intimidating. They had decided not to worry about the object on Darwin's back. It was not painful or hindering; they would have to deal with it later. *If we actually survive this*, she lamented.

Clouds had been rolling overhead for the last hour. Dot thought he heard thunder somewhere off in the distance. *Rain would be very bad today*, Blurr thought despairingly.

Ralph joined the others, and they all swooped in low over the sheet of glacial ice. Blurr scowled as a wave of frigid air hit her in the face. It was a deep chill and made her muscles recoil and she could not wait to be away from it.

They landed just past the ice on a large boulder near the entrance. Darwin hopped down to the edge of the hole. It was large enough for Pshotee to pass as long they folded their wings and went one at a time. The ground around the edge was worn with lots of foot traffic. Blurr could smell the strong scent of decaying vegetation waft up from the dark cavity.

Like two searchlights, Darwin's large glowing eyes peered down the mouth of the cave; his head was completely engulfed as if the cave itself were swallowing him whole.

Everyone stood silently waiting; swiftly, he withdrew and looked at Dot. Blurr and Ralph were used to this by now, knowing Darwin's look when he was communicating with the owl directly.

"The first part of the cave is empty," Dot said. "Though his connection with the Pshotee has lessened, he senses that they are deep within the cave, at the center."

"I still don't like the idea of you going with him," Blurr said seriously.

"I don't either," Dot responded. "But if Darwin can't get the queen to follow him or is killed, then we lose big time. You won't get your chance. Darwin says that we will be used only if he fails."

Blurr couldn't think of another plan of action. Dot was right that she couldn't navigate the cave without Darwin's help and she needed to be out in the open prepared for the queen if she came out.

Ralph clumsily landed next to Darwin. "We better go," he said, and without hesitating, he stepped into the darkness and disappeared. Dot shrugged and followed him. Darwin lingered a moment and stared at Blurr. She looked deeply into the blank glow of blue then said, "Don't fail, Darwin, please."

He stared back, his lips moved as if he was going to try to speak but stopped as if he thought better of it; instead, he bowed low with eyes closed then squeezed into the hole and was gone.

∞

Dot was disoriented at first within the cold catacombs of earth. Though he had night vision, this blackness was pure and impenetrable. He could hear Darwin entering the cave and suddenly, the blueprint of the tunnel was clear in his mind. They moved with confidence, easily avoiding obstacles of tripping roots and sections of low-hung ceiling. Additionally, shadows of the rough texture of earth appeared as the glow of Darwin's eyes gave just a faint hint of bluish hue to the immediate area.

"It's getting wider," Ralph whispered from up ahead. Dot couldn't see him but heard his rapid breathing and once he heard the tapping of Ralph's nervous foot stomping. Dot reflected on the fact that Ralph led the way into the cave despite his fear; it was the bravest thing he'd ever seen his friend do. He brimmed with pride at that moment like a parent over a child's sign of maturation.

Dot felt the walls withdraw; he clung to one side and crept along. After a few seconds, he whispered hoarsely, "Does it feel warm to you all of a sudden?" The stench of rotting leaves was stronger and accentuated with an unidentifiable putrescence.

Darwin was still behind Dot when a vision of a drop-off emerged in their heads. "I see some light ahead, Dot," Ralph breathed.

Dot stopped abruptly. "Ralph!" he hissed. "Don't move!"

A low light appeared directly in front of them. Dot realized it was the same glow that Darwin's eyes gave from behind them, only the light ahead was much greater.

Ralph froze, waiting for direction. He sensed that Dot was listening to Darwin in the silence, though he couldn't be sure. Finally, Dot broke the quiet. "We're here."

∞

Darwin eased through the tunnel, stepping over Dot and around Ralph until he came to the ledge of a long drop into an abyss. Dot and Ralph huddled behind him and peered into an immense cavern.

"There are so many," Ralph said in a hushed tone. It reminded Dot of stars twinkling in the night.

Brilliant radiance of hundreds of pairs of glowing blue eyes illuminated the giant cavern. Dot could see large earthly walls with stone ledges on which dark masses of Pshotee clung. They were packed together vying for space, constantly clamoring over their neighbors. The cave was full with the echoes of clicks and shrills as the Pshotee communicated to each other.

Dot observed that these Pshotee seemed more vicious than Darwin; maybe it was because he had grown to trust him or maybe freedom from his queen's mind allowed him to have his own personality. Dot wasn't sure; all he knew for certain was that he was terrified of the image before him.

At that moment, Dot's mind felt as if it had been doused by icy water. He froze with a shudder as a voice pierced his thoughts, *Thank you for bringing my servant back to me.* It breathed like an ill wind whispering images into his head. Dot immediately felt sapped of strength; his limbs sagged as Ralph turned back with a face of "are you all right?"

Dot couldn't move, then another flood of thought streamed through his mind. This one was clear and defiant. *You cannot have me!* Dot realized that Darwin was breaking into Dot's mind and confronting the queen. He felt the weakness of his limbs subside as the queen's attention was drawn away but could still hear distant echoes of the conflicting dialogue between the two minds.

You will always be mine, she said soothingly. *You know this to be true.*

You're wrong, Darwin shot back. *I will never be yours again, and neither will anyone else!*

You cannot destroy me, slave! she hissed. Dot could feel the queen's anger rising.

Maybe not, Darwin said defiantly, *but I know one who can!*

The owl's mind saw a vision of Blurr float through lazily and then vanish. Instantly, the cavern was filled with an ear-piercing shriek; it echoed off the walls and sunk deep into the heads of Dot and Ralph, both of whom recoiled, losing their balance and falling to their sides. The queen seemed to be laughing viciously, *I killed all the small ones you call falcons when I first awoke. They are small and insignificant, none of them would have a chance at challenging me.* To this Darwin simply replied, *You missed one.*

∞

Ralph and Dot sat limply at the opening of the cavern when Darwin flared his wings and leapt off the ledge and into the void of somber blue light. Echoes of many screams were heard. Dot and Ralph could not see anything at this point; the ringing in their ears left them disoriented.

Dot's mind cleared quickly now that both the queen and Darwin were out of range or at least focused on something else. "Ralph!" he called, not worrying about secrecy any longer. "Can you move?"

"That hurt," Ralph strained, "but I can move."

Ralph was crawling toward Dot when, without warning, the blue glow of the main cavern was shrouded by a dark figure; Darwin stood in the opening, looking winded.

"Darwin says," Dot translated, "the queen accepted the challenge but left through a crevice in the ice that he did not know about. She has already set out to find Blurr!"

Just then, a wave of hundreds of high-pitched screams resonated throughout the cave as a rushing torrent of beating wings filled the space. For the first time ever, Darwin spoke aloud in a low and clear voice marred only by the pronunciation given his mouth full of teeth. "Dey are comink, fwiends, we wust go!"

"You spoke!" Dot squeaked. "I didn't know you could actually say something, you know, without invading my head."

"I hab bin pwaticing when you an Raf are aswip," Darwin struggled but was visibly proud of himself.

Ralph patted Darwin on the back with a wing just as the first of the Pshotee began inching through the tunnel.

With a wave of panic, the three companions began to hop and run through the tunnel as fast as they could, knowing that the horde of Pshotee had just been called to battle and were right behind them.

Chapter 24

The Inner Demon

Blurr had been waiting for what seemed like eternity for her friends to come out of the dark hole. She found a rock ledge further up the mountainside where she had a good vantage point. Rolling storm clouds accumulated with sickening strength. *Ki'ta will be here soon*, she thought.

The surrounding forest was quiet, just as she remembered the night she first met the Pshotee. She tensed; her feathers bristled. She could sense that her part was to be played out soon. Muscles twitching, she adjusted her feet, remaining focused on the cave entrance, expecting either her friends or her enemy to be coming out any moment.

She felt a breeze brush against her back; whether it was because she was so jumpy or something told her to move she did not know, but at that moment, she flushed off the branch. At the same instant, in the place where she was just perched, a dark and sinister figure appeared, crashing against the branch, snapping it clean away.

The face resembled Darwin's to a point, dark with a snout and a leaf-shaped nose at the end, but then, the jaw flared out like a snake's. Its eyes were blank but burned white-hot while the mouth slid open and hissed to reveal true snake fangs, dripping with a clear secretion.

It swerved toward Blurr; its body dripping with a black tar that sprayed in droplets in all directions as it flapped gigantic black membranous wings.

A long thin tail flicked as the monster adjusted its approach. "You are the one I seek," the queen seethed in the common language. "I have seen you in the mind of my slave."

As she spoke, both black tar and clear fluid issued from her mouth; Blurr smelled rotten flesh drift into her nostrils. She felt repulsed by the vile creature and was tempted to retreat as fear crept into her very marrow. She steadied her flight and looked back. "I am she," Blurr screamed, "the one who is going to kill you!"

The queen hissed and lurched after her, striking with lightning-quick jerks of a long flexible neck. White eyes tracked every move with hatred. "You and your kind will not defeat me this time!" she screamed.

Blurr maneuvered in all directions, trying to get her to follow into the open sky where she would make her attack. The queen was fast, but not as fast as the falcon; a glimmer of relief and confidence soothed her nerves. *At least I can stay at a safe distance*, she thought, *until I'm ready.*

There was still daylight left even though the sun had descended behind the mountains, but the ensuing storm clouds that rolled into thick blankets of gray drowned out the afternoon rays. It was getting darker fast. Blurr stole a glance behind her, checking to make sure the queen was still in pursuit, only to be struck by a horrific sight. She was gone.

At a loss, Blurr banked left and circled back down, retracing her path. She flew, just grazing below the low-lying clouds; wind gusts were throwing her off balance and sweeping her into the cloud bank. She felt like the wind and clouds were working together to corral her. The momentary loss of visibility was frustrating, and she had to force herself not to panic; she had lost complete track of the queen and wasn't sure what to do.

Just before she cleared the clouds, her side suddenly burned as if stabbed by a hot spike. She winced and twirled; her wings tried to maintain flight, but she couldn't control them and she began to drop.

She fell out of the clouds; her body was paralyzed but burning as if she were ablaze. She looked up to see the massive dark shadow of the queen materialize out of the cloud bank. She could see the white eyes watching satisfyingly as Blurr plummeted to the ground.

Blurr's heart sank; she had failed. She didn't even have the chance to give a good fight. She was angry at herself for allowing the enemy to ambush her and sad that her failure would lead to Ki'ta's doom.

Her body throbbed in pulsating waves of heated pain; she was now looking forward to the impact of the ground, hoping it would put an end to her misery. However, it did not come. Instead, a soft bed of black feathers inched its way underneath her, and she sensed her descent begin to slow. She still couldn't move; the pounding heat waves were excruciating and it was hard to process anything else, though she did notice another dark shadow similar to the queen's but smaller come into view. Darwin's glowing blue eyes were staring back at her; his face was etched in deep regret.

Blurr's vision went out of focus; her head swam with images that she did not recognize. She saw the stars, but not from the ground or the sky; instead they were all around her. There was no ground or trees or clouds, only stars and never-ending blackness. Then the images changed. With the visions came feelings of sadness and loneliness and anger. Blurr realized that these feelings were not her own but the feelings of another, whose memories she was witnessing. She now saw a dark landscape; a rock and a tree lay before her, and it was cold.

Blurr couldn't tell whose memories they were, nor did it seem that she had any control over the situation. Her perspective was low to the ground, and she could see black ooze coating the ground around her. She felt the need to consume, but she didn't know what. Suddenly, the dark sky was peppered with rapidly moving animals flying in a group over her. She reached out with a dark, dripping tendril and caught one. It squirmed and tried to bite the black ooze that ensnared it. She felt nothing but satisfaction as she drained the life from the small bat.

Blurr's visionary self was content, like after a meal. But it wasn't hunger that was satisfied but knowledge gained from the tiny creature. She now felt whole and able to become more solid. The black ooze pulled back, and she grew, limbs spreading, dripping out to each side. She had to really concentrate on the form or it would melt back to the oily liquid. She longed for more knowledge. Her immense wings unfolded; the knowledge from the bat gave her instruction on what to do next. She flapped hard until she was high in the night sky.

The images changed again. This time, the loneliness was unbearable. She bit many creatures from this world, but none developed fully. Most died in the change, while others only half developed and went wild with madness, flying or running away into the night.

Then she felt content again. There was a creature before her; this time, Blurr recognized it as a Pshotee. It looked like Darwin, but it bore no emotion or sign of intelligence. She could feel that her loneliness was subsiding; suddenly, there was hope.

She saw flashes of people screaming and changing, and each time, she was happier but felt weaker. The vision swirled again and formed a scene of many birds of prey chasing her and her followers off land and across vast open expanses of water. Feelings of revenge and hate consumed her; she would have to make more to destroy those that would oppose her. Her hate boiled deep within her soul; it drove her to consume many humans until she was almost utterly spent. She was pleased that the two-legged hairless animals were so conducive to changing into her soldiers. The task of changing so many had exhausted her, and she must sleep; they all must sleep until her strength returned and she could destroy all in her path to dominate this new world.

The series of images was fading, replaced by concerned voices. She let her focus shift to the familiar sounds; the images now vaporizing to nothingness.

"Blurr, can you hear me?" said one voice.

"What is happening to her?" replied the other.

She tried to remember who she was, but it was difficult; the voices sounded familiar, but she was having trouble picturing to whom they belonged.

She heard a third voice, but it was strange because she wasn't exactly hearing it through her ears, the words just seemed to be appearing in her mind. *She did not receive a full bite, but it was enough to cause some change in her.*

"No!" screamed the first voice.

As Blurr's awareness of herself crept back into memory, she realized that her body no longer felt like it was on fire. She opened her eyes. The faces above her were engulfed in a thin wisp of glowing energy. She also noticed that even the trees and plants in the background were dipped in this same golden light. Her body felt whole and unscathed, even stronger than before. She did not understand but at the moment, was too grateful to not be dead to question what had happened.

Dot, Ralph, and Darwin surrounded her body. "Am I alive?" she asked, looking into their stunned faces. She did not recognize her voice; it had dropped in pitch and was not birdlike but sounded like many voices speaking in unison.

Both birds nodded dumbly. Blurr saw Darwin look upon her with curious eyes, watching her closely. "Can you move?" Dot said shakily.

Blurr tried and found that she could move quite easily. She hopped to her feet, surprised at her strength and speed. She gaped as she saw the world now in full view; every living thing was surrounded in a golden aura. "What is wrong with my eyes?" she said aloud, shaking her head to see if that would somehow correct them.

Her friends stood beside her, speechless. She realized that they were on the ground, all three still staring at her, not moving.

"Blurr," Dot said, "I don't really know how to tell you this." He paused and approached her, still fixed on her face. "Darwin saw your wound and . . . it was made by the queen."

"Yes, Dot," Blurr chimed, "I think I know that!"

"Right," Dot continued, "well, when something is bitten and is not killed, they . . ."

"They what!?" Blurr said impatiently.

"They change."

"I found one here," Ralph said, standing fifty feet away.

Dot and Darwin lead Blurr to where Ralph was standing; there was a small clear pool of water left by a miniscule stream trickling quietly down the slope. She peered into the water and saw her reflection.

She stood in shock. Her legs felt unsteady as her mind whirled at the sight of her face, for instead of her dark brown eyes, there was a pair of glowing blue eyes, blank of any pupil or iris.

"No!" she breathed.

"Darwin says that you did not fully transform because you did not receive a full dose or her venom," Dot explained. "He does not know what else might happen."

Blurr quickly checked the rest of her body. Nothing else seemed to have changed. Grateful, at least, to find that she still had a falcon's body and face, she turned to the others.

"Where's the queen now?" she asked hastily, calming the anger that swelled within.

Before anyone could answer, a far off cry echoed among the storm clouds above. Blurr, Dot, Ralph, and Darwin looked up into the darkening sky and saw hundreds of specks peppering the horizon; the raptors were grouped in clusters with some flying low while others flew higher, just underneath the ceiling of clouds.

As if in reply to the hawk's cry of challenge, a high-pitched shriek drowned out the call of Ki'ta, the small band on the ground traced the shriek to directly above them. A massive army of dark-winged Pshotee flew in tight groups; the queen was leading them.

"The battle has begun," Blurr cried and leapt into the air. Dot, Ralph, and Darwin followed close behind her, but soon, she was out-distancing them. Her focus was on the queen.

She scrambled under the horde of dark beasts; the Pshotee army did not notice her as they all flew robotically toward the army of raptors. Blurr was gaining distance on the queen; she could see the slick body and larger wings beating the air furiously just up ahead. Then she saw Ki'ta leading her hawks directly toward the queen and her horde. *No!* Blurr screamed in her head. *Don't attack her. Go for the others*!

At that moment, Blurr saw Ki'ta motion to her right and left and the group divided, swerved, and looped around the queen and directly into the front line of Pshotee, leaving the Queen zooming unchallenged through the opening.

Could she have heard me? Blurr thought. There wasn't any time to ponder the coincidence as the two armies clashed with tremendous ferocity.

Bursts of feathers exploded in the evening sky and floated down like snowfall. Screams of pain and cries of battle were heard all around Blurr. The melee was mesmerizing as bodies slammed into each other; the sounds of ripping and tearing of flesh were everywhere. Her adrenaline flowing, she picked her first quarry; the Pshotee saw her and locked on her as well.

She swiveled her body slightly and collided with the furry beast. Her small last-minute adjustment allowed her to avoid the snapping jaws of her opponent and she felt bones crack on impact. She pushed away as the body of her enemy slumped, flapped feebly, then fell limply into the dark green forest below. Immediately, two more were converging on her. She banked left and dropped a few feet, narrowly escaping a claw swipe from one of her pursuers. She banked straight up and looped. It was like her body had taken over control. There were so many of them to avoid, she couldn't think fast enough. Her instinct was now steering her body to barely miss being struck by tooth or claw.

She glanced back to see the two Pshotee hunting her get hit by two eagles. The bodies rolled and twisted. One eagle managed to free himself, leaving the Pshotee ripped and falling. The other eagle was still entangled with the giant Pshotee and both tumbled into the forest below.

"No!" screamed the eagle as he shot past, trailing his fallen comrade into the canopy of trees.

Blurr dove too but was impeded by a large group of Pshotee coming straight for her. Just then, a host of large owls flanked her without a sound. "These are ours, falcon!" Boldree hooted joyfully. "You can go find your own."

∞

It seemed like only seconds had passed since the first moments of battle. Blurr had no sense of time; she felt supercharged. She noticed with her new vision that her acuity was doubled, details of her surroundings were cast in light made by hundreds of auras of birds, Pshotee, and the landscape of so many living things. She sensed that she could track movements of others easier than before as well. It was as if she could anticipate the movements of anyone that she happened to be focused upon.

She scanned the skies and saw that the Pshotee were overwhelming the raptor army.

She sighted the queen. She had just disposed of two eagles, their limp bodies hurtling through the battle, knocking others to the ground. Blurr bolted for her, dodging Pshotee and raptor alike. *I must get to the queen.*

She was nearing the queen when she caught sight of Ki'ta; the hawk was in a gripped lock with a Pshotee and tumbling out of control. *Let go, Ki'ta, you're almost to the trees!* she thought. Suddenly, Ki'ta pushed away just as the first branches reached up to ensnare her. She twisted and swooped to the side, narrowly avoiding them while the Pshotee plunged directly on a spike-like branch near the top of the tree.

Blurr breathed in relief and turned back toward the queen, only to find that she had disappeared. She scanned quickly and found the snakelike head zeroing in on Ki'ta. Instantly, Blurr zoomed toward the monster. She saw that Ki'ta was unaware of the queen's approach as she fought against two Pshotee that were attempting to keep her attention focused away from the queen.

It happened in an instant. One pass of the dripping body and dark wings and suddenly Ki'ta was falling toward the earth. "Not her!" Blurr screamed aloud.

The white-hot eyes swiveled back and locked on Blurr. The queen's face was that of surprise; she whirled around to face the falcon. Blurr's mind was filled with pure rage; she felt that the aura around her body was seeping into her. It shimmered like sunlight dancing on water. She felt her wings stretch and enlarge, her body elongating. Her feathers laid flat and smoothed into a glossy skin. Her face smoothed and stretched as well while her beak morphed into a giant jowl with rows of brilliant white teeth.

She let out a cry that rumbled like thunder. Members of both armies stopped in midbattle to see what made the bellow. All watched as Blurr, in her new form, rushed the queen.

The great black body of the queen coiled and hissed as she lowered her head, fangs poised and clawed feet bared. The two flying titans clashed together, a boom echoing throughout the skies. Both bodies were tangled and writhing, moving with lightning speed and wicked viciousness.

Pshotee and raptors hovered in awe as the two behemoths fell to the ground, both only focused on ripping the other. Suddenly, as if renewed with purpose, one eagle sounded a war cry and charged a Pshotee; instantly, the rest of the raptor army sounded the call. The Pshotee began to scatter and retreat with hawks, eagles, and owls trailing them.

Boldree looked back to see that the queen and her giant mysterious opponent had disappeared.

Chapter 25

Crushing Blow

"Did you just see what I just saw?" Dot stated numbly from a treetop.

"I did," Ralph replied. "But I don't believe it!"

Dot and Ralph were perched on a tall cottonwood tree watching the battle. They had decided that little owls and cowardly vultures would not do well in such fights, and so they watched at a safe distance. Darwin had left them soon after Blurr departed abruptly to go after the queen; he said that he had an idea but did not linger to tell them what he was going to do.

They had lost track of Darwin in the throng, being that he looked much like all the other Pshotee. Blurr stood out, however, as she was the only falcon in the melee. Not even the common kestrel, smallest of the falcons, was present. They had watched her zoom in and out of Pshotee and then later transform right in front of their eyes.

"Darwin was right," Dot mumbled. "Something did change in Blurr."

"Yeah," Ralph muttered then swiveled his pink head toward Dot. "But is it still *our* Blurr?"

"I hope so, buddy," Dot said quietly. "That thing was huge, and deadly."

The two friends looked on in moments of trepidation, waiting to see if their friend was going to resurface. But to their dismay, it wasn't so. Suddenly, a dark shadow burst from the canopy of trees into the twilight; its huge membranous wings opened as the terrifying face screamed in victory. Immediately, the horde of retreating Pshotee reformed into tight groups and swung a sharp angle directly toward the pursuing raptors. The return of the queen had rekindled the vicious fire of destruction; the Pshotee seemed more organized and more dangerous than before.

Screams rang out in the night as swarms of Pshotee were overwhelming raptors of all kinds. Eagles, owls, hawks, even a small regiment of osprey had joined the battle but were being torn apart. This new charge led by the insidious queen and the defeat of Blurr had spelled doom for any remaining raptors. Any birds left in the sky began to frantically retreat but were relentlessly dogged by Pshotee ripping feather and wing.

The queen had already killed several birds when two Pshotee suddenly lurched in midair then fell limply to the earth. She looked in all directions for this mystery assailant but found none. Perplexed, she hovered, fluttering her giant wings and scanning the sky. The problem was that there wasn't any other animal within attacking distance.

Just then, the Pshotee only feet in front of her jolted to one side, then whirled uncontrollably into the abyss of dark countryside. The queen now noticed that other Pshotee soldiers were randomly falling as they chased the raptors into submission.

∞

"Good shot, Johnson!" Fitzpatrick yelled as he fired two more shots into the sky. The four FBI agents stood with braced footing as they held their pistols high into the air.

"Remember," Patricia Nelson said, "go for the big one, we take that one out and the rest will scatter!"

"Got it, chief!" Fitzpatrick said, holding his semiautomatic pistol aloft. He still wore his cowboy hat but held his weapon with the traditional two hands that all FBI are trained to do.

Patricia Nelson was in a corner. The situation had deteriorated to following the advice of a telepathic enlarged bat who originally was a person. She was sure her report to the main office about these things would appear ludicrous, and she would be sent to an insane asylum.

"Tell me again what this giant bat intends to do if the leader is killed?" Patricia yelled, firing three blasts in rapid succession. She had always been a good shot on the firing range, but rarely were her targets fluttering about like dancing butterflies hundreds of feet in the air. One of her shots made its mark; the bat slunk and fell like a dead leaf.

"He told me that the largest of the Pshotee is the leader," Erin cried as she crouched behind a tree, holding a set of metallic rods that looked like old TV antennas from a house's roof. "And if she were to be destroyed, he could get control of the others and would disappear away from people."

Patricia Nelson had a hard time believing that Dr. Simms could speak to these creatures, but then, if she could communicate with it and the thing was telling the truth, then maybe together they could contain the situation. At this point, she realized that this was no ordinary circumstance, one that had to follow a regiment of procedures that had been trained into her over her years of service. This was a nightmare, and if a floppy-eared bat the size of her mastiff says the big lady dies and they go away, then so be it. She aimed another shot at the biggest monster in the sky, but only got a smaller one just in front of her.

"These things are fast!" cried Millman as she sent a Pshotee into the trees.

The FBI, with Erin's help, had tracked Darwin using radio telemetry. Erin had fixed a small radio transmitter to his back hoping to keep tabs on his location. No one had any idea they would be walking into a bloody battle of birds of prey and giant bats.

∞

Fitzpatrick brought his pistol to his hip and loaded it with another magazine; he stole a glance at Zoe Millman standing near him, taking aim and firing twice. "So is anyone going to admit they saw one of those birdies change into a big flying . . ."

"Dragon," Mike Johnson finished. The agents all stopped discharging their weapons and lowered them but kept the barrels pointed outward. They gaped at Johnson who had frozen in his firing stance silently but remained fixedly looking into the sky. In the still of the night, in the midst of clouds of smoke from dozens of rounds of gunfire, Mike Johnson, ex-football star, FBI veteran, and a stone-cold soldier, whispered, "I like dragons."

"I like dragons better than I like those slime ball devil birds up there," Fitzpatrick muttered.

"Did anyone see it come up from those trees?" Millman asked hopefully. They all shook their heads.

Nelson, Erin, and Daniel scanned the sky for survivors and for the possible return of the queen's rival who disappeared into the forest. "I think I've got something," Erin murmured in the dark.

"She's got Darwin's signal," Daniel said softly as he sat next to her, monitoring the black box resting on the ground.

"Whatever he's going to do," Nelson voiced, looking through her binoculars hopelessly as all she could see at this point was darkness, "he had better do it soon, it's awfully quiet up there, and last I saw, there weren't many birds left."

Erin held up her hand and breathed. "He's close!"

Just then, Darwin swooped over the heads of the FBI agents dragging in tow several Pshotee and two dozen ravens. Last to follow was a smaller Pshotee whose flight line was awkward but enthusiastic. Daniel stood, recognizing his friend and shouted, "Go get'em, Sherm!"

The FBI agents holstered their weapons; Patricia Nelson had done all that she could to assist a plan derived mostly by animals. It was too dark to fire their weapons anymore; she looked up into the starless night, shaking her head. On top of everything else, it looked like it was going to rain.

∞

Sherman was trailing the line of ravens; he was getting better at his Vulcan mind-melding, as he called it. *I must have been crazy to agree to join you,* he sent to Darwin.

This is a battle not only for birds but also for the Pshotee, Darwin sent back from the front of the pack. *Besides, I thought you might be able to convince the ravens to join us.*

I said I thought I might know a way just because I know that ravens like shiny stuff, Sherman transmitted to Darwin.

So what did you say that convinced these ravens to fly with us in the pitch of night? Darwin asked amusingly. Even though Sherman was breathing hard, he was finding it remarkably easy to carry on a casual conversation mentally. He was becoming more comfortable with the Pshotee ways of communicating and even lamented at how wonderful it would have been to have this ability as a human when he would jog on the town's bike trails trying to pick up women.

Well, first of all, talking aloud with all these teeth is not easy, Sherman said mentally, *but eventually, I told them that my friends could get them my old Christmas tree decorations from my apartment. They went wild. Listen, are you sure these are the same ravens that tied you up a while back? They don't seem that bright to have managed such a thing.*

The thoughts from Sherman's mind barely left his head when Darwin's reply flooded back. *Yes, and don't remind me of that humiliating day and don't underestimate what a few ravens can accomplish when they have nothing pressing to do!*

Sherman looked up ahead, his night vision was awesome, and he enjoyed not being blind by the night anymore. He could see the ravens fanning out, but pairs of birds were holding something in their feet, connecting them like a pair of children holding a jump rope waiting for someone to plunge in for a go.

"Okay," Dad commanded, "Right, you take the left flank with Milten, Earl, Scruffy, and–"

"That makes no sense," Right protested. "Why wouldn't I take the right flank, after all, Dad, I'm Right!"

"Right!" Dad said without hesitation. "You take the right flank while Left takes the left flank with Jasper, Mumbler, and Carmine."

"Raven sandwich?" Left asked with intense excitement.

Dad smiled, and they zoomed off into the night.

By now, the sun had dropped below the mountains, and the sky had changed to night. Stars were obscured as the clouds had now fully entrenched themselves. The first raindrops began to fall.

∞

The mystery of losing several of her soldiers was not solved but had stopped since the last rays of light vanished. She continued to try to find the source of this new power, but her attention was drawn to a new enemy. Her rogue soldier had come to challenge her. It was no matter, the last of the raptors were surrounded; her horde encircling them in the air, not allowing them to leave. She intended to watch them exhaust themselves in the rain and drop to their deaths.

She peered at the lone soldier flying directly at her. *You have failed, my child*, she soothed. *Come back to me, come back to your brothers and sisters, come back to your family.*

You are not my family. You took me and my family and made them your slaves! Darwin charged, still hundreds of feet away from the horde and the doomed raptors.

I made you my family, for I had lost mine and my world, the queen whimpered as her head coiled snakelike, ready to strike. *I came to this world and was met only with loneliness and despair and aggression from those vile birds!* This time, the honey-sweet voice sharpened to a growl as it entered Darwin's head.

Raindrops fell from the dark clouds; Darwin knew his time was running short. The surviving raptors and his ravens weren't going to last long with soaked feathers.

The queen also realized this and screamed triumphantly; her horde echoing her cries of victory. As if to sink the final blow, the queen's blank white eyes narrowed in concentration as her soft membranous ears twitched rapidly. Suddenly, raptors of all kinds began to voluntarily dive toward the wet ground. Some were low enough that they had already made impact. Others who had managed to still have enough strength were now screaming as they plummeted downward.

For the first time since he had changed into a Pshotee, Darwin opened his huge mouth and roared into the night like a lion challenging all comers. The queen looked on in relish as she controlled the minds of the diving raptors but whose face suddenly changed as the one Pshotee turned into two, then four, then eight! Pshotee were fanning out to the right and left of Darwin, presenting a single file line of very angry looking faces.

The queen's eyes narrowed, her concentration refocused on Darwin. In that moment, many raptors pulled out of their suicidal dives, narrowly missing the ground. The encircling Pshotee scattered and reformed behind the queen.

Without warning, there was a sudden cry from above. Several of the queen's Pshotee looked up just in time to be clotheslined by pairs of ravens zooming straight downward as they dragged vines between them. She hissed bitterly as she watched many of her soldiers get clipped or fully entangled in the mesh of vines, falling and crashing into the forest below.

She looked up to Darwin who was still coming straight for her; his followers were now engaged in aerial battles with opposing Pshotee. She was livid and was set on killing Darwin.

Come to me, child, and meet your fate! she hissed and coiled her neck once again preparing for Darwin's relentless charge.

∞

The FBI and Erin and Daniel had sought cover in the trees when the cold rain began to come down in violent sheets; they had left their cars in a parking lot at the trailhead and had hiked for at least thirty minutes to get to a vantage point to see their target. Now, they were blind as well. Erin was holding up her radio telemetry antenna hoping to get some indication of where Darwin had gone. The others listened to the action in the sky from underneath pine boughs; the storm made it difficult to see, yet occasionally, dark silhouettes of birds and giant bats zoomed in and out of focus.

"Something just happened," Johnson said in a grave tone, listening to the echo of a roar that was soon drowned out by the rain. Zoe Millman stood close beside him, trying to stay as dry as possible. She looked out from under a branch and saw an object crash land in a set of bushes only feet from them. Instantly, the four agents drew their weapons, aiming them at the bush. Branches jostled, and a large dark mass came crawling out of one side. Two glowing blue eyes stared at them in the dark.

"Don't shoot!" Erin shouted. "Its Sherman!"

Daniel immediately got up and ran to the limp creature. "Are you hurt, Sherm?"

The soft glow of Sherman's eyes cast Daniel's face in relief. "I heard him this time," he cried. "He says he's okay, that Darwin has gotten reinforcements, and that they're heading toward the lake."

"What lake?" Nelson blurted, her rain slicker shiny with wet.

"Leigh Lake," Daniel announced. "He says that Darwin just got the thought pattern of someone named Blurr who had changed into a giant and something about the queen hating water and this Blurr will take care of things." All heads were staring blankly at Daniel. He caught their eye, declaring, "Well, okay, I can't hear everything he's telling me, but I am getting better!"

"The dragon's back!" Millman exclaimed.

"Looks like we're going to get even more wet, folks," Nelson stated from within her hood. "We need to know this thing is finished, we need to know who wins this fight to make our next move. All right everybody, let's move!"

There was some grumbling as people came from out of the shelter of the trees and clicked on their headlamps to find the trail. Soon they were all standing in a line waiting for Daniel who was kneeling next to Sherman on the ground; a moment later, Daniel stood up and joined the line. "Is he going to be okay?" Erin asked softly.

Erin's headlamp shone a bright light into Daniel's face; he winced and said with a toothy grin, "I think he's going to be just fine."

They began to trudge down the trail. Fitzpatrick blurted, "I've got twenty dollars on the dragon, any takers?"

Chapter 26

Avenging Angel

Blurr stood, her scaled legs wobbly, but the impact of hitting the ground was beginning to wear off. She felt her long neck swivel; her enormous wings extend and whip-like tail lash against the rain. She marveled at how the rain didn't affect her; she was warm and did not feel wet or even uncomfortable. The water droplets rolled down her body; her scales were like armor.

She saw the queen and the Pshotee amassing, then she saw the last of her brethren dive into bush and tree. *They weren't landing of their own accord!* She remembered the day she witnessed Darwin controlling the two nest guard hawks, convincing them to go to Ki'ta to allow them to speak. She thought of Ki'ta and renewed anger welled within her. *This is not over,* she thought determinedly.

Blurr rose into the air with her new body; flashes of lightning lit up the clouds like an X-ray. She roared to the heavens and pumped her giant wings, gaining speed. She raced after the queen and her horde as they headed toward a large mountain baring a dark column of rock jutting out of the side like a great turret on a castle. The mountain was familiar to her; she realized that the queen was going back to her nest.

Do you remember the lake at the foot of the mountain, Blurr? entered a whispering thought.

"Darwin?" Blurr said, surprised. Her enlarged beak and mouth full of teeth made it more difficult to use the common tongue she noticed.

Tis I, you must meet me at the lake, Darwin went on. *You must take her into the lake by force. If she is split, she may not be able to pull herself back together in such cold waters.*

At the foot of Mount Moran sat a serene lake, cold and deep. It was surrounded by pine forests and under the night and clouds looked like a black hole in the earth. Blurr's powerful new wings surged her forward at incredible speed; if she could dive with this body, she would be unstoppable.

She angled up, now flying high in the cloud cover above the queen's horde who was, to her surprise, dealing with a group of determined ravens, and she couldn't help but notice that there were scatterings of Pshotee battling other Pshotee. She smiled inwardly, thinking of Darwin.

She knew what she must do, and this time, she wasn't going to fail.

Blurr came out of the ashen clouds to see the queen directly below her, with the black lake spanning in all directions. She tilted downward, but just as she did, the queen looked up and screamed a high-pitched wail. Immediately, she swerved, heading back to land, but before she could get there, the monstrous body of the queen shuddered for an instant.

Blurr knew her moment had come; her target was still, and her line was direct. Tucking her wings, she dove.

Her large body plowed through the gooey center of the queen; she felt the warm ooze coat her body. It stung and bit at her; she watched the two halves of the queen fall into the dark lake with a loud splash.

Blurr tried to stay aloft, but the tarlike goo gripped her wings close to her body, and she too fell, plunging into the icy abyss along with the queen.

Only a little distance away, six people stood on the lake's edge, all were holding cell phones high above their heads, the eerie glow of each phone's wallpaper image shining faintly. "I didn't think the cell phone thing would work," Fitzpatrick said, still holding his phone up in the air.

"Darwin said it might have some effect," Erin uttered lowering her arm.

Waves, made by the three large objects hitting the water, lapped the gravelly shore at their feet.

"Hey, guys," Fitzpatrick say jovially, "I think it's stopped raining!"

Chapter 27

Parting of Friends

The air was still. Leigh Lake was like glass, reflecting Mount Moran with a perfect inverted image. A mist hung over the water as a merganser calmly led her brood through the still water. The sunlight was warm on Blurr's back as she lay facedown on the pebbly beach. Her limbs were stiff and her mind fuzzy. She opened her eyes to see a black beetle amble along its way peacefully just an inch from her face. She watched it curiously; she thought how nice it must be to live a worry-free life, to just crawl and live and not have life get so complicated.

"She's waking up!" Ralph said excitedly, his foot stomping the pebbles rapidly.

"Give her some space!" Dot commanded as he approached near her. "Blurr? Are you okay?"

Blurr breathed loudly. She tried to respond but her body was so exhausted she couldn't even speak. She nodded her head slightly, crunching gravel under her cheek. She could hear her friends become excited then Dot said, "Can I help you up?"

Blurr nodded again. Both Ralph and Dot did their best to hoist Blurr's body up to a standing position. They found it hard, though, to keep her upright as she kept sliding sideways. For the first time, Blurr opened her eyes fully and gazed down at her body. She was expecting the large dark shape she had taken form of the night before, but instead, she looked upon her old body, the body of a peregrine falcon.

"You changed back!" Dot squeaked. "Well, except for the eyes, they still look like Darwin's," he added.

"I think I can stand on my own," Blurr said, holding herself steady. Suddenly, images of the battle and the events of the night before exploded in her mind, ending with the fall of Ki'ta. "My sister!" she exclaimed.

"Don't worry," Dot said quickly. "Ki'ta is all right, apart from the broken wing."

"But I saw the queen, she . . ."

"She didn't get a bite," Dot finished, "if that's what you mean, but Ki'ta took a hit and is grounded."

"And the queen?" Blurr asked tentatively.

"Well," Dot said, looking at the lake, "two of you went into the water, and only one of you came out."

Blurr was overwhelmed with relief; she roused her feathers while trying to process the fact that the queen was gone and Ki'ta was still alive and was not going to change into something like what she had become. This notion did not sit well. She was an outcast before; what did this change inside of her make her now? Even if she did find other peregrine falcons, would they accept her? Would anyone accept her as she was?

"Blurr," Dot said quietly, "maybe we should go to Ki'ta, she was asking for you."

Blurr wanted to go, but she suddenly remembered that her eyes were sure to give her away of the infection she had incurred; she was not a pure raptor anymore. She was afraid that Ki'ta would shun her, maybe even consider her an enemy. Dot and Ralph urged her to follow them; she reluctantly leapt into the air and trailed behind them. The scene of clear skies, green forests, mountains, and a calm lake below was so different than the raging torrent of the night before.

"Just in those trees over there," Dot said while Ralph soared over them.

Just then, Blurr saw an odd sight; several humans standing on a beach at the water's edge, and they looked like they were talking, a line of Pshotee standing nearby. She tensed, ready for an attack when Ralph swooped in from above. "That's Darwin, he's talking to the humans about Ki'ta."

This was getting more confusing by the second. "Why would he be talking with humans about Ki'ta?" she asked loudly.

"The woman, Erin is her name, she heals animals," Dot chimed happily. "She's going to heal Ki'ta if the hawk will let her. That's where you come in Blurr."

"Me?" Blurr exclaimed. "Why would I try to convince Ki'ta to go with a human?"

"You know what a life would be like for a hawk with a broken wing," Dot said. "The clan could not take care of her, she would die."

Blurr was getting closer to the scene; she could see six humans standing in a semicircle around Darwin with at least twenty Pshotee lined up behind him. "I don't understand."

"Darwin can talk to humans," Dot said, "especially the woman, Erin. He has asked her to help, and she said she would."

"And the others?" Blurr asked suspiciously.

"No idea," Dot said casually.

They flew over the beach and soon arrived at a clearing within the pine forest. Blurr saw Ki'ta standing proudly on a log only a foot off the ground; her wing was cocked in an unnatural way as it dragged low at her side. Many hawks, eagles, and owls were perched nearby.

Blurr landed in front of Ki'ta. "I'm glad you are alive," Ki'ta said formally.

"As I am glad you are alive," Blurr replied as formally as she could muster, her voice still sounding like chimes. She watched as Ki'ta looked over her approvingly.

"I have heard that you vanquished the queen." Ki'ta continued, "For this, I will be always grateful."

"I am honored to have helped such a strong and wise clan as yours . . . sister," Blurr said, bowing low.

"Your eyes are different," Ki'ta said, but this time the formal tone had been dropped, replaced with more sentiment. "But I still see my sister in them."

Blurr's heart burst with joy. "My sister, I would like to ask a favor in return for the part I played last night."

Ki'ta looked down. "I am grounded and thus bound to death, but if I can, I will honor your request."

"I would ask that you go with the human," Blurr said, looking into Ki'ta's amber eyes, "and allow her to heal you so that you can return to your rightful place, as *rital* of the hawk clan."

Several of the raptors perching nearby fidgeted at Blurr's request; some looked abashed at the thought of going with a human in place of death on the ground. But Ki'ta just stood still; her face unwavering as she stared back at Blurr's glowing blue eyes. "If this deed, unto whatever end, repays the valor you showed my clan last night, then I will do it."

Blurr smiled as well as Dot and Ralph. There were some protests from other birds, but she did not hear them, and apparently Ki'ta refused to listen as well. The sisters just looked at each other in a peaceful moment of understanding.

∞

Blurr watched as the humans took Ki'ta away in a cage; she felt sad to see her confined. She knew how that felt and how Ki'ta had felt about a bird being in a cage. She hoped Ki'ta would heal quickly. Soon, only she, Dot, Ralph, and Darwin were left on the beach. A small breeze had begun, lapping waves rhythmically next to them. It was a clear day with no clouds; the sun was already heating the sand under their feet.

I must be going soon, Darwin voiced his thoughts into their minds.

"But where will you go?" Blurr asked.

I have explained to the humans that the Pshotee have named me as leader, Darwin vibrated. *They will have the chance to think and feel and maybe remember who they were, to have our individuality back. The woman, Erin, has helped me locate a place far from here, a place called Alaska, where the Pshotee can live in peace. She said that as long as we stayed away from humans, no one would come looking for us.*

"What about Sherman, or is it Batman?" Dot asked.

He said he wants to be called Sherman again. Darwin vibrated. *He thought Batman was a stupid name, and he thinks that if he ever changed back to a human, it would be easier to keep his old name. Sherman decided to go with us, I think he is beginning to feel like one of us, and he needs a family.*

"Will we ever see you again, Darwin?" Dot squeaked pathetically. He was trying to not show his affection but was miserably failing.

Darwin looked down at the little owl. "You neva know, litta ol, I hop our pads cwoss again," he said aloud grinning his rows of white fangs.

Without warning, Ralph stepped in and wrapped his huge black wings around Darwin, the vulture's head buried somewhere in Darwin's shoulder. Ralph's shoulders were throbbing as huge muffled sobs could be heard through the Pshotee's fur.

They said their last good-byes, and soon, Darwin was gone, back to retrieve his new family and take them far off. Blurr had to admit that she was sad to see him go; she was starting to like him but knew that being with family meant everything. She wished him well.

The beach was deserted except for the three friends. "Well," Dot hummed, "now what are we going to do?"

"I'm hungry, Dot," Ralph whined. "Let's find a nice dead animal."

"You forget, my friend," Dot said happily, "we have a new and improved falcon. We can have anything we want, right?" The yellow eyes of the saw-whet owl looked up encouragingly to Blurr.

Blurr's eyes were blank of expression now, but she found herself rolling her eyes in complete surrender. These were her friends, for better or for worse.

A month had passed since the day the queen went into the lake. There were no more sightings of Pshotee and the raptor clans were fanning out into their territory once more. Blurr had stuck with Dot and Ralph but was increasingly feeling restless. She enjoyed their company but longed to journey out into the world to find more of her kind. She wanted to learn the traditions and culture of her race of falcon and maybe find out why they were so scarce.

"Maybe you're the last one of your kind," Dot had said casually one day.

"Come to think of it," Ralph added, "I've never seen anything but those tiny kestrels around here."

"I must see if there are more peregrines out there," Blurr said, trying not to offend her friends. "If there are, I must find them."

"When will you be leaving us then?" Dot said, choking back tears.

"Not until the big day," Blurr responded, trying to console her little friend.

"That's only three days from now!" Ralph said alarmed.

The next three days were spent visiting all the places that Blurr and Dot and Ralph had spent time. They told stories and even ran into Dad, Right, and Left making the largest nest they had ever seen. It was full of shiny string, and loads of Christmas ornaments and something called tinsel that Sherman had given them. Dad was disappointed to find that Blurr's falconer bells she had when they had first met were gone. *Funny*, Blurr thought, *I didn't even notice.*

At last, the third day had arrived and all three friends ventured to the top of a barren hill just outside of the human town. Blurr perched in a lone stunted pine tree far from the gathering of people on the hilltop. Dot and Ralph went in much closer; the humans Erin and Daniel set iron perches for Dot and Ralph to rest on right beside the crowd.

Next came a host of people. Blurr recognized two other faces in the crowd. A serious looking woman with short graying hair and a man with a large black cowboy hat stood nearby watching as a dog's kennel was brought to the forefront of the small crowd of people.

The voices hushed as Erin approached the cage. Blurr watched as the human said words to the other humans, none of which she could understand, then bent down and reached into the cage.

The crowd applauded as Erin stood up with Ki'ta wrapped in a drape; her beak was the only thing visible as it protruded out of the edge of the cloth. Daniel approached from the side as Erin adjusted her grip under the cloth. She faced Ki'ta outward, and with a fluid motion, Daniel pulled the drape back, revealing Ki'ta's face wild with surprise. Erin spread her feet and threw Ki'ta away from her, the drape falling limply to the ground.

Ki'ta cried a long high-pitched shriek that echoed off the hill side. Again the crowd applauded as Blurr watched Ki'ta flap her wings mightily and make a long circle over the crowd looking down at Erin. Blurr watched Erin wave, then Ki'ta banked left and flew high into the clear blue sky.

It is time for me to go, Blurr thought, sitting on the lone tree. She saw Dot and Ralph entranced with the festivities; they seemed to be enjoying all the attention they were getting from the humans taking their picture. She thought about saying good-bye to Ki'ta but decided against it. Ki'ta would have to focus on reclaiming her place as the *rital*; they would see each other again, maybe next summer.

Her glowing blue eyes ablaze with anticipation, Blurr lit off the branch and rose into the blue sky. The air was colder, and she could sense that summer was over; soon this land would be brown then covered in snow for the long winter. She would go far; she would find others of her race, and hopefully, she will find her own family.

THE END

Edwards Brothers Malloy
Thorofare, NJ USA
April 12, 2012